HERS TO CALL

Dria Andersen

Dedication

To my husband who was my sounding board, my cheerleader, my critique partner, and all the things I needed to finish this project. I appreciate every hour, every word of input and most of all, your unwavering support.

To my family who had to deal with mommy being in another world for hours at a time. Thank you for your patience.

To my sister Tina, who reads everything I write and gives me honest feedback and encouragement, thank you mucho mucho. I appreciate your continued support and cheerleading!

Thank you to every fan who continues to stick with me while I tell the stories playing in my head. I appreciate each and every one of you.

Table of Contents

- 1 -... 1

- 2 -... 12

- 3 -... 21

- 4 —.. 37

- 5 —.. 53

- 6 -... 68

- 7 —.. 81

- 8 —.. 89

- 9 —.. 100

- 10 —.. 110

- 11 —.. 119

- 12 —.. 135

- 13 —.. 149

- 14 —.. 157

- 15 —.. 164

- 16 – 178

- 17 - 191

- 18 - 204

- 19 - 211

- 20 - 218

Epilogue 229

About the Author 234

Other titles by Dria Andersen 235

$$- 1 -$$

Simon Jacobs now believed in destiny. It was as much a part of him as his heritage, a gift, no doubt, from his mother. His father—a self-proclaimed practical person— would've brushed the sentiment aside, telling him his bear would lead him in all things. In this case, either of them could've been in the right. His bear had chosen its mate, and whether or not fate had put her in his path was irrelevant at this point. Five years ago, hell, maybe even a year ago he'd have dismissed any talk of destiny. He'd wanted to believe he had control in all things, but it had taken a simple glance at Calita Wright, and just a small hint of her scent for his bear to rip that delusion from him.

He sighed, his body buzzing from just the memory of that day. He'd come to Selena's diner on a whim, searching for something sweet. He had spotted a woman as she talked with his cousin's wife Selena, their heads bent together at the counter. His bear had rumbled, tightening his body with power until half the patrons had turned to him, their gazes curious. Calita's soft voice had reached his exceptional hearing and yearning clouded his mind. Only the iron control he asserted over his bear had kept the creature from bursting from his skin and rushing to her side. For her safety and his sanity, he'd left the diner that day.

But, he had come back.

Often.

And prayed fervently, sending thanks to the gods his mother and their people worshipped. He and his bear, waited. Waited and plotted on the best way to secure their mate. Bears were nothing if not patient, and as the alpha, he had more patience than most. His bear had grown impatient with his pace, though, but Simon wouldn't be rushed. Not when he saw flashes of fear in Calita's gaze when she thought no one watched her.

Watching her skitter away from people, Simon had worried at first that she had an issue with shifters. But, he'd come to find out that Calita shied away more from the humans. Especially the males. Her nervous glances, the little flicker of her tongue as she moistened her lips, he catalogued it all. Calita was a little skittish, no doubt about it. But eventually, he would have her, he held no doubts about that either.

Last night he'd decided that his bear was right, it was time to make a move on her. It was one of the reasons he'd picked the comfortable booth he currently occupied, instead of the one nearer to the back of the diner in which he normally sat. He sipped his coffee and flipped through the Sunday paper, his hooded gaze watching the human wife of one of his bears.

"Mornin', Alpha."

"Good morning, Selena."

"You gonna say something to her today?" Selena settled a hand on her generous hips and gave him a sly look.

"You keeping a calendar I don't know about?" He folded the newspaper and laid it on the table.

She smiled. "You been in here for dinner two weeks straight, hiding in that back booth, watching my girl." She wiggled her eyebrows." She wiggled her eyebrows.

He stifled his smile. Nosy bears. Calita was the first human to catch his eye, so he understood their fascination. Mating with humans was no strange thing, yet as alpha, it had always been believed he'd mate with a shifter. He'd grown up in a time where humans in Bear Ridge were rare, and it was rarer still for them to interact with each other. He'd never once considered a human for his mate. But, his bear had chosen, and that was that, so he gave it no second thought. He knew his clan would be the same, so he allowed them their fun.

Now that a new treaty with the humans was in place and the immediate threat of government interference in their town gone, his bears deserved the frivolity of teasing their alpha.

Behind Selena's light banter, concern for her friend lurked in her dark brown eyes. Her gaze roved his face, searching for something. "Calita's not like…"

He inclined his head. "She's your friend. I understand, Selena."

"I mean no disrespect, Alpha." She paused, her gaze lowering.

"She's been hurt." It wasn't a question. Calita had a natural wariness that told more than words could.

He'd figured out some months back that his mate had been through something. It was the only reason he'd been able to leash his bear for so long. Impatient though they were, the two of them were in agreement that hurting Calita was out of the question.

Selena sighed. "Some, but that's for her to tell."

"When have you known me to mistreat a woman?"

She let out a hard breath. "You're right."

"I'm always right." It was an automatic answer, his bear prickling at the thought of someone thinking Simon wouldn't take care of their mate.

She lifted her hands and barked out a laugh. "Fine, I'll leave it be. Besides, another week of you tiptoeing will earn me a hundred dollars."

He had to laugh at that. "The sheriff know you up in here gambling?"

"You let me take care of the sheriff." She winked, a twinkle in her eye at the mention of her mate. Her face straightened, and her gaze drifted to the door. "Speaking of Calita."

Selena hadn't needed to tell him. His bear rose and Simon closed his eyes as her scent reached him. The warm fragrance of cream and honey hit his senses, and hunger assailed him. The familiar sound of her footfalls reached him next, and both he and his bear went on alert. It was rare to see her in the diner before lunch, but there she was. Her long legs, and thick thighs encased in a pair of fitted jeans that did wonders for her ass. The simple, no nonsense V-necked blouse clung to her, outlining her full breasts. He was entranced, his gaze following her as if by compulsion. His body buzzed, and his head spun with need gripping him.

Not now, she'll be ours soon. He placated his bear, pushing down on his power.

Simon's gaze traced her face, seeing the signs of a sleepless night in the dark circles marring the brown skin under her eyes. His jaw clenched and his grip tightened on his coffee cup. He wanted to walk up to her, demand she rest and let him take care of her. Instead, he could only follow her march towards the kitchen with his eyes. Her long black hair was tied at the nape of her neck, twisted into one of those nonchalant buns she liked. He'd only caught one glimpse of her hair down, and the image was burned into his brain. Her cocoa skin was smooth and unadorned. No make-up, no jewelry, nothing to detract from her natural beauty.

Her heart shaped face was serious as her eyes occasionally looked up and darted across the diner. She had a wary way about her. That look a deer got in its eyes when it knew the hunter was close. That momentary flare of panic that widened the eyes and kept the body on alert. He wondered, not for the first time, what his mate was running from. He'd given her time to settle in, but from the rumble leaving his throat, his bear was done with waiting. Selena chuckled and touched his shoulder as she left him.

Simon thought on it as he sipped his coffee. His mind wondered back to why she'd come in so early. He didn't usually see her. Not that he came to breakfast every morning, he had work on the ranch that kept him busy most days. There were some days, though, when he had a hankering for the pastries Calita made…that and he craved the sight of her. He came often enough that it had raised the town's interest, even though he wasn't the only one drawn into the diner by the pastries and desserts Calita made. Bears who almost never left their dens and bears from miles away had started making the trek to Selena's diner.

But, he would admit…

He'd given himself away from his first glance of Calita.

And now everyone in town was betting on when he'd make his move. He shook his head and waved down a waitress to order a dozen more of the croissants with lemon jelly to go. He'd hide them in his office and hope his second in command didn't sniff them out before the day was done.

The small diner was starting to get crowded as the patrons of the small hotel next door trickled in. Most of those patrons would be headed out to his ranch once breakfast was done. Watson Ranch was a big tourist draw for their town and he was extremely proud of that. It was a reminder that he had work he needed to be doing. But taking his mind off his mate was harder with each passing day. Calita was a mystery he was intent on solving. He thought it best to wait until the shadows left her eyes, but a year in their small town and she still seemed tense and uneasy. Obviously waiting would get him nowhere with this particular problem, so he needed to take action.

Besides, if he didn't say something in the next couple of days his Beta threatened to do him bodily harm. Gavin wanted to win the money from the pool. Simon shook his head. He liked seeing his bears happy. Even if it was at his expense.

***

The kitchen was busy, the loud noise music to Calita's ears. The staff was small, but efficient, good-natured insults were tossed back and forth in easy camaraderie. The diner where she now worked was small and a far cry from the fancy restaurant in Chicago where she'd been executive chef, and she got far more enjoyment from it because of that. Selena had hired her to take over the kitchen, but she'd felt more comfortable assisting her friend, getting a feel for the place. She didn't want to…no couldn't, deal with the extra responsibility when she'd first arrived. But recently, even though she kept the schedule of a line cook, Selena had moved all responsibility over to her. Calita's lips quirked up into a smile. They were both obstinate, she would continue pretending to be a regular kitchen employee, and Selena would steadily defer decisions to her until she caved.

The breakfast crowd was coming in steady streams, and Calita was happy she'd come down earlier. She should've been upstairs trying to get more sleep before her shift, but she'd found that working helped keep the demons away. Remnants of her nightmare flitted across her mind. Her hand lifted, pressing against her shirt, just under her bra, her habit of rubbing the spot, reflexive. She needed to feel the scars that were proof of nightmares made real, it was compulsion.

The kitchen door swung inwards and her best friend since middle school sauntered in, a mischievous smile covering her face. Calita jerked her hand from her chest and changed her gloves, going back to work on her dough.

Cali shook her head. "I don't trust that look in your eyes, Lena."

"What look?" Her friend leaned against the stainless-steel table Cali worked at.

She waved her spoon at her closest friend. "That look, the smug one you're wearing."

Selena waggled her neatly arched eyebrows. "Someone has an admirer." She fluttered her lashes, her voice rising an octave.

Cali shook her head. It was a good idea for her to leave men alone for a while. But, that would explain the feeling of eyes on her she'd felt when she was walking through the diner a moment ago.

"What's new? Ms. Thang keeps them panting after her." One of the waitresses waited at the window for her order.

"It's not me, personally. I'm sure it's because I'm new here." Cali set down her spoon and dumped her dough onto the pastry mat, avoiding Selena's eyes.

"Yeah, okay." The waitress grabbed her tray and closed the pickup window with a laugh.

Calita chanced a look at her friend and noticed she still wore her smile. "You're up to something."

Selena shrugged, but arched her eyebrows. The smile on her face dropped when she got a good look at Calita's face. "What's happened?"

"Nightmare." She raised her hands as Selena gasped. "I'm handling it."

"If you need to talk."

"Really, Lena, I'm fine, I just need…" she shook her head. "You've given me what I needed." She whispered. "A fresh start, a place where I finally feel safe. Give it time."

She looked around, not wanting the others to hear the strain in her voice. Selena touched her shoulder and nodded. Calita kept herself from flinching from the touch. With the nightmare fresh on her mind, she was anxious, agitated. But she noticed since she'd come to Bear Ridge that people did that a lot.

Touch.

She'd finally trained herself not to flinch.

Yay her.

She puffed out a breath and pushed down the need to escape her friend's probing stare.

Selena cleared her throat. "Is that why you're down so early?"

"Yes."

"You've gotten, what, three hours of sleep, tops." Selena brushed a hand over her hair.

"I'll be fine. I'll go upstairs and take a nap before I start the desserts for dinner. Besides, you're lucky I came down. The pastries for breakfast are low anyway."

"Well, you know bears."

Calita nodded. Another thing she was learning since being here, the appetite of bears. Wasn't life funny? Shifters had come out to the public decades ago, and she didn't think she'd met a single one until she'd come to Georgia.

"Don't you want to know who it is?" Selena asked, changing the subject.

Calita sighed, wishing her friend had changed it to something else. "I do not."

Though, she was a little curious. The men around this town were hunky to say the least. She didn't know how she felt about dating a shifter. She'd arrived at the town wary, thinking they would be dangerous animals, but the human she was running from had scared her way more than that possibility. From day one though, the gentle bears had made her feel safer than she had in a long time. Even through their curiosity, they'd given her space. They passed along compliments on her cooking, or gossip about town and its people, all the while never intruding into her personal space. It had made her feel welcome.

Selena leaned over the counter and opened the pickup window, jarring Cali from her thoughts. Her best friend pointed to a man sitting alone at the booth directly across from them. Calita's nape tingled, her body tightened and her breath stalled. Her eyes collided with a set of onyx ones. Heat flooded her cheeks, her stomach did a lazy flip and her body awakened. *Who was he?* She blinked to break contact. A mocking smile tilted his full lips and he raised his glass of juice in a toast. How had she missed a man that fine?

My God.

He couldn't be real. High cheekbones, hollowed cheeks and a squared jaw gave him a rugged look that pulled at her feminine core. Curly hair flowed to his shoulder in wild disarray, along with rich dark copper skin. Was he Chicasaw like the majority of the town? Maybe also Black? Thick eyebrows lowered over those dark eyes as his heated gaze roved her face. Feminine awareness and a healthy dose of self-preservation had her moving out of view of the window. All that restrained power crackling around him, *Lord*…just a look at him had Calita's hormones bouncing around her body. Her hands shook as she went back to kneading.

Who was he?

Not her business. She couldn't afford the promise of heat in his eyes.

Selena laughed outright. "So, you want to know his name?"

Yes.

She shook her head no, still unable to speak. She was shaken, but not in a bad way.

"Simon's a great guy," Selena sang.

Feminine sighs met that statement. Cali narrowed her eyes at the staff. The town's alpha. She'd heard a fair amount of stories about him and they did nothing to prepare her for the dominance that radiated from the man.

Intense.

That was a better word for it. She turned to the sink and washed her hands to give herself a moment.

"That man is a God," someone said.

"You ain't never lied." This from one of the prep chefs.

"Thank you for disrupting the kitchen," Cali accused.

Selena shrugged her rounded shoulders. "If you don't want him, I can think of at least a dozen women who'll take him off your hands."

Bawdy laughter had her rolling her eyes. "Whatever. You can leave now." She turned back to the table.

"Make him work for it, Cali." Another waitress said floating past her, tying on an apron.

Cali swept everyone in the kitchen with a stern gaze. Chuckles met her look. "Disrespectful, the whole lot of you," she teased. "Back to work. I'm not talking about this."

She shook her head and promptly ignored them. She couldn't shake those dark eyes though. Upturned at the ends, mysterious, and heated, his gaze would haunt her. Selena left the kitchen laughing. Calita puffed out a breath, her hands shaking until finally, the others lapsed into busy silence.

Simon…yeah, she wasn't ready for that.

$$- 2 -$$

Steam followed Calita as she stepped out of the bathtub, onto the thick carpet, wrapping a fluffy towel around her chest tightly. She'd taken a break around two, after the lunch rush. That was to say, Selena had kicked her out of the kitchen a little while ago with instructions to rest. Not hardly. She caught a glimpse of herself in the bathroom mirror as she adjusted her towel and her heart skipped a beat. She dropped the towel, standing naked in front of the mirror, studying her body. Calita was tall, five ten in her bare feet. She wished she was a little smaller, skinnier, more like what David said he wanted. The only way she would be smaller was if she starved herself. It wouldn't happen. Though the years after her attack had weened her down from the size she'd used to be. She traced a hand over her mahogany skin, gliding over the soft flesh, only stalling when she reached an area that was raised, smoother than all the other skin around it.

The scars were not as bad as she imagined they'd be. Not as jagged as her nightmares made them to be. He'd been precise when he cut into her skin, the small fillet knife leaving just enough of a scar to remind her of his sadism. Calita traced the small scars crisscrossing below her breasts. Hate for her ex-boyfriend bloomed, along with anger that she was still frightened of him. He'd been on the run from the police for the last three years and she was still having a hard time getting over it. She'd wasted away in Chicago, barely leaving her house, fear trapping her.

PTSD, Post-Traumatic Stress Disorder, they'd called it.

She sighed and turned away from her reflection, tightening her towel across her chest. She was doing well here. Selena had come to see her in Chicago and urged her to come down. Selena had said there was something healing about the town and she wasn't lying. Last year before Calita had arrived at Bear Ridge, seeing her scars would've sent her to bed for the rest of the day.

Progress.

She was proud of herself. Looking at the clock, she got dressed. She still had time to take a little bit of a walk before she went back for the dinner shift. She quickly threw on a clean pair of jeans and a black V-neck t-shirt, her normal uniform for when she worked in the kitchen. A comfortable pair of trainers went on last and Calita took the stairs down three floors to the lobby.

She slowed as she spotted Simon chatting with the front desk clerk; she scrambled to remember the young girl's name. Tessa, maybe? Calita had kept to herself in the year since she'd been in Bear Ridge, hardly speaking to anyone outside of the restaurant staff. She needed to be better about that. She put it out of her mind as Simon straightened and looked back at her. His gaze raked over Calita in a way that felt possessive, covetous. He certainly hadn't earned that level of familiarity. Why then did her body stir at the attention?

She gave him what she hoped looked like a smile.

"Hi," he turned and greeted, waiting at the desk.

She patted her hair and lowered her gaze. "Hi. You're not waiting around here for me, are you?" She narrowed her eyes. She should feel scared, but somehow, she couldn't even work up alarm.

"Perhaps." He walked over and held out his hand. "I'm Simon."

She stared at his hand for a long moment. Lifting her eyes to meet his eyes, she found she couldn't keep his gaze long. Her hand was trembling as she held it out. The calluses on his palm scraped across her skin, the warmth of his skin sent a thrill through her and she reveled in the strength in his hands.

"Nice to meet you, I'm Calita."

He smiled again and she was struck by how beautiful the man was. Like really, he shouldn't be able to send her heart soaring from a smile. She felt like she'd accomplished something just by getting him to smile. She cleared her throat and her stray thoughts.

"So…" she clasped her hands in front of her.

He shook his head and smiled. "I'm sorry, I had a whole host of clever and charming lines to say to you when I finally talked to you, but then you came down the stairs, and well…"

Okay, she was charmed by that. She ducked her head to hide her pleasure at his words.

"Can I join you on your break?"

"Well, I…" she looked around unable to find an excuse and quite frankly not wanting to. "Sure. I was just going to step outside for a little sun."

He nodded and motioned for her to lead the way. They walked in silence along the sidewalk headed towards Bear Ridge's downtown city proper. Squat brick buildings lined the sidewalk, their large windows showcasing each store's wares. Small magnolia trees were spaced along the walk, providing them with shade, while the flowers scented the air around them. Cars moved along the street next to them at a sedate pace, no one seemingly in a rush.

She'd really fallen in love with the small town. It was time for her to come out of the shell she'd built around herself.

She sneaked a look at Simon. Opening up to the townspeople was one thing, dating again was a whole other thing.

***

Simon walked along with Calita, happy to spend some time with his mate. He should've been working. There were guests aplenty at his dude ranch, and yet he'd barely gotten five miles outside of the city before he turned his truck around to get back closer to her. He'd called the ranch and told them he was running errands. Seeing right through the excuse, his Beta had simply snorted and rattled off a list of supplies they needed. The back of his truck was full from his visit to the hardware and feed store, but it would keep until he was ready to leave.

Calita had him nervous. That was new. With every step he took with her, every notion he had about how his mating would go was tossed aside. Finally close to her, her sweet manner and soft voice had him reconsidering his carefully laid plans. How did the span of ten minutes in her presence shift his priorities so thoroughly?

"How do you like the city?" He finally broke their silence.

She smiled, and his bear purred, rolling over.

"City is a stretch." A dimple appeared in her cheek. "But, it's charming, much like its residents."

He gave a small chuckle. "You're an amazing chef, by the way."

She touched her chest. "Thank you."

"I can't be the first person to tell you that."

Her smile got a little sad. "No. But I've found genuine pleasure feeding the bears in this town. They're a lot more appreciative than I'm used to."

He nodded, knowing his bears had never had an issue with saying how they felt. "We try."

They continued in silence, passing through the town square. He returned waves from his bears and rolled his eyes at their thumbs up. His gaze drifted back to Calita, skimming the features of her face. He couldn't wait until she was his to touch and savor. His bear rumbled in agreement.

She turned her head to him and smiled shyly. "You're staring."

"You're beautiful."

Calita her head the other way, but not fast enough to hide her smile. "I thought you were out of clever lines."

He laughed. "I'm not used to having to come up with flowery sentiments. I'm a straightforward person, a simple bear. I know what I want, and I go after it."

Her pulse sped at her neck. And she kept her gaze straight ahead. "And what is it you want?"

He paused walking and waited until she stopped moving.

"You want pretty words, or do you want a straightforward answer?"

She swallowed and turned her gaze to him. "I'm not much for pretty words myself."

A woman after his own heart. He inclined his head. "You're new to shifters and I understand that. Humans have a different culture than shifters, would you agree?"

She crossed her arms over her chest. "I would."

He stared at her, noticing that she avoided his eyes. Not that that was strange. Most people, shifter or human alike, couldn't keep eye contact with an alpha. That wouldn't change until they'd fully mated.

"I want you."

She sucked in a breath. Her eyes darting to his before sliding away.

"I know that once with you would never be enough." He decided to leave his bear out of the equation for now.

"You're just going to lay that out there?" Cali blinked in surprise, the pulse at her neck thundering. "and I'm supposed to… what?"

He smiled, unable to help it. She was so beautiful. He stepped a little closer to her, not quite getting in her space, but allowing the heat from his bear to envelope their mate. He stuffed his hands in his pocket and made his pose as non-threatening as possible. "Take it how you want, Calita, but I can guarantee you would love every minute of it."

Calita eyed him, her face showing her astonishment. "You can't just go around telling people you want them." She protested.

Her outrage shouldn't amuse him, but he was finding her bafflement charming. "See, here's where we run into those cultural differences."

"I don't have the time or energy for a relationship," Calita said, but her eyes and body language told a different story. She was tempted, it was in every shuddering breath she took.

He pushed at another button, wanting to put his flustered mate a little off balance. "I'm not talking about a relationship yet, Calita. I'm talking about hot and intense, consensual sex." Simon stepped back and let her digest that.

Her lips parted in shock and Simon balled his fists in his pocket to keep himself from leaning over and sampling her full lips.

"How about I make you an offer? You can have complete control. You come to me when you want me or call me to you. Either way, you control the time and the place. I'm yours to call, whenever you want." Hell, for this woman he'd do whatever it took. Wait as long as he needed for that ultimate prize.

"You would settle for a booty call," she attempted an aloof look, but her heated gaze raked his body.

Simon lifted an eyebrow and tilted his head, his gaze skimming over her fine ass. "I mean…"

"You're desperate," she said.

"Decisive," he corrected.

"That simple, huh?"

"There is nothing simple about the things I want to do to your body." He stepped a smaller bit closer, his bear clawing at his chest. "From the moment I saw you, my heart stuttered. My bear…" he breathed out a rough breath. "You're a fantasy come to life."

She scoffed, "You got all that from a glance?"

She was shocked, that was clear. But, her scent drifted to him on the breeze and there was no mistaking her interest in him. The pulse at her throat beat a rapid tattoo against her skin. He thought on his talk with Selena and knew he'd have to take it slow with her. Where the hell the offer came from, he didn't know. One moment he was walking with his mate getting to know her, and the next thing he knew, the horny bear in him decided to challenge its mate. It was a dangerous game, one he was nervous they'd lose. His bear had no such qualms. So, he put his trust in the animal, knowing its instincts had never failed them before.

Her hands shook as she patted the top of her head, which he'd noticed was her nervous gesture. He would back off for now; give her some time to think.

He smiled. "It's a simple offer, Calita. You now know how I feel. Take some time, think about how you feel. When you know, come find me."

"And if I agree to this?" She whispered.

"Then I will give you the ride of your life."

He intertwined their fingers and brought her hand up. He kissed the inside of her wrist, inhaling her fragrance and committing it to memory. She sucked in a breath and he hid his smile. Yeah, she was interested. He would leave now before she could work herself into offended.

"Here is my number." He gave her a card from the ranch, he'd written his cell number on the back. "Call me anytime. Even if it's not about this, and you just want to talk, you hear?"

She nodded. Her tongue darted out and licked her bottom lip. "You would let me control the sex?"

"No, I let you control when and where. The how…" he paused, "The how, we figure out together."

"No strings?" She looked surprised at her own question.

"None." At least none for now.

"If I say no?" she tested.

"You're in control, Calita." Not an answer, but he didn't want to lie to his mate.

Her lips pursed in a moue of concentration, but she didn't call him on it. Simon decided he had pushed enough. Yeah, he should leave before he leaned over and took the kiss his bear was clawing at him to take.

"Call me."

She nodded, her face a mask of concentration. He waved and turned away from her before his bear could push him into something Calita wasn't ready for.

$$- 3 -$$

Morning was always a busy time on a ranch the size of the one Simon owned. Various clan members were working, giving him funny looks as they passed. Normally, Simon was interacting with them, checking in to make sure everything was running smoothly. This morning though, he was stuck in his head, so he understood the looks. He led the horse he was riding by the reins, his mind on the offer he'd made Calita yesterday. It was all he'd been able to think about all morning, really.

"Yo, Earth to Alpha." Gavin, his foreman, and second in command waved his hand near Simon's face.

Simon shook his head and gave Gavin his attention.

"Did you hear anything I just said?"

"I'm sorry, Gavin, I missed it."

"You've been distracted all morning." Gavin took off his hat and wiped his forehead. "Not a good thing around the horses."

Simon grunted at the admonishment.

"Would it have anything to do with the lovely chef?"

"None of your business," he muttered.

Gavin laughed. "There's talk of you two walking around the city holding hands, getting chummy."

"We were not holding hands." A petty point, Simon knew.

"Either way I lost the bet. I was sure it would take you a couple more days."

Simon sighed. "Hopefully with the bet over, the town will stay out of my love life."

"Not likely," Gavin chuckled.

Simon slapped his horse's flank and sent him into the pasture with the other horses awaiting riders for the midmorning trail ride. "I'm going to get lunch and pretending I don't know that my bears are cooking up another bet."

Gavin's laughter chased him into the house. He'd lost a lot of time this morning woolgathering. Time he'd have to make up after lunch. He sighed. He would eat quickly and get back to it. There were two families checking in the next day and he mentally went over his checklist to make sure their cabins are ready. He stomped his feet off at the back door knowing Becca, the she-bear who looked after his house, would fuss if he came in with dirty feet. He usually entered the house through the mud room in the garage, but it was one more thing to chalk up to distraction.

"Hey, Becca, I'm just home for a few minutes to eat." His voice trailed off as he looked up and spotted his ex-wife sitting at his kitchen table.

He darted a questioning gaze at Becca and raised his eyebrow. She huffed and set his plate on the table.

"My mama raised me right," is all she said.

Simon read between the lines. She didn't like it, but Becca would not be rude to his unexpected guest.

Simon sat and said a prayer over his lunch, his daddy's habits ingrained in him even years after the man was gone. The hot roast beef sandwich smelled good. "I praise the day you came into my life, Becca." Simon said appreciatively.

She rolled her eyes and went back to cleaning the countertops.

He took a bite of his sandwich and stared at his ex-wife. Miranda was still beautiful, in an artful, put together way. Her hair, auburn, straight and silky stopped at her shoulders and complimented her caramel skin well. Last time he saw her it was black and cut into a sleek bob. Simon couldn't help comparing her to Calita. His ex-wife was petite, even elfin in appearance, where Cali was tall, and all soft curves. Miranda's dark brown eyes were hard, cunning, a plan almost always brewing in the back of her mind. Of course, when they were married, Simon thought of it as determination, strength, especially when it came to fighting for shifters. He'd admired her, plain and simple. Now, he saw the calculation he'd glossed over before. Her eyes couldn't compare to Calita's warm and expressive ones.

"What do want, Miranda?" he asked minutes later, now that the edge of hunger was appeased, he hoped it would help control his temper and his bear.

"You've really turned the farm around," she commented.

Her tone was nonchalant, but he could see her mental calculator tallying the changes he'd made and fixing a price to them. If he let her, the hard sell would start. There was always a cause or organization that needed just a few more dollars to 'really get their mission going'. Simon continued eating; she'd never needed prodding to talk.

"Aren't you going to ask me how I'm doing?"

"Miranda, I only have a few minutes to eat lunch, I don't want to spend it playing games with you."

"Alpha, if you don't need me, I'll excuse myself and go help get the cabins ready for our guests tomorrow," Becca broke in, giving Miranda a nasty look.

"I'm fine, Becca, thank you," Simon smiled at his self-appointed housekeeper.

She was very protective of him. But then, she had been there when his wife decided she didn't like country or clan life and left him, taking the majority of their savings and cleaning out their checking account. Thank God he hadn't had access to the clan's funds at the time. She probably would have run off with that as well. He'd had to console himself with the thought that at least it would go to some grassroots organization. Miranda had never had use for money outside of that.

"I came to apologize, Simon." Miranda lowered her voice and lounged in the chair in what he was sure she thought was an enticing pose.

"Not needed, you can leave." Simon stood and gathered his plate.

He placed it gently in the sink, wrestling his temper. He leaned back against the counter and crossed his arms over his chest. Now that the smell of roast beef wasn't in front of him, Miranda's scent floated to him, astringent and sharp. He wrinkled his nose, *what was she wearing?* Even as a hybrid, Miranda's sense of smell should've prevented her from wearing whatever perfume she'd put on.

"Look, Simon, I know the way everything ended—"

"Don't, Miranda." Simon clenched his jaw. "Make sure you're not here when I return."

He left the kitchen, careful not to slam the door on his way out. The last thing he wanted to do was show Miranda that she could still get under his skin. Five years later and she still had the power to anger him. He stomped from the house, determined to put her out of his head.

"I just need a few minutes of your time, Simon," Miranda called from behind him.

He suppressed a growl and turned back to face his ex-wife.

They had only been married for two years when his father became ill, two rocky years. The marriage hadn't survived their move to rural Georgia, nor the responsibilities Simon had put on his shoulders. Caring for his father and taking over a failing horse farm and a clan in disarray from an ailing alpha had been time consuming. Time Miranda hadn't wanted to spare.

"What could you possibly have to say to me after all this time?" Simon bit out.

"You know how the life is. I need a place to lay low." She stared into his eyes defiantly, before the compulsion to lower them overrode her obstinacy.

Revolution was the life she spoke of, and he knew it well.

He'd left home at eighteen and joined the fight for shifter liberation. Protesting had not been for him, he'd not been interested in a peaceful resolution. His father had been content with the scrap of land the government had given them to live on. Joseph had led their clan as best he could with the stingy resources they'd been allotted. Simon had refused to stay on the sanctuary and eke out a living the way his family had for decades.

He felt he could help better on the front lines. It was where he'd met Miranda. Every time Simon had thought of coming back home to the bear Sanctuary, anger had gripped him, no doubt fed by his militant wife. She'd fought for shifter freedom as strongly as he had.

"You come here, to the people you gave your ass to kiss and ask for a place to hide?" Hands on his hips, he could only stare at the audacity of Miranda.

When he'd gotten the call about his ailing father, Simon had given no thought to packing up the life he and Miranda had made in Atlanta and moving back to Bear Ridge. Miranda, on the other hand, had kicked and screamed the whole way. She didn't want to cater to the needs of a chaotic clan and she certainly didn't want the responsibilities that came with being an alpha female. Once Miranda realized the clan had no interest in her revolution, she'd turned her attention elsewhere.

"I'm not built for the life you wanted." She waved her arms at the expanse of his farm.

"You mean you didn't want to work for it. Now you come here for what…refuge?" Simon closed the distance between them, anger burning through him.

She growled, the light of her bear brightening her eyes. "I don't know why I ever try to talk to you. You never listen."

Simon sucked in a sharp breath, aggravated and frustrated at Miranda's usual refrain. "What do you expect from me? You sent divorce papers the same day I buried my father." He hissed.

She gasped and stepped back, her face blanching. "That's not…it was never my intention to hurt you like that."

He raked a hand through his hair disgusted that he'd fallen into old habits with her. Arguing with his ex-wife was not how he wanted to spend his morning.

"I can't have you here, Miranda. I have a mate now." At least he would once he could convince Calita. His ex-wife had no right to that information though.

"I'm not asking to live here, for Christ's sake, I just need to lay low for a while." She snapped. "She would never even notice me on a ranch this size."

Simon shrugged, his stance unmoved. Besides the fact that he didn't want Miranda on his land, he wouldn't risk even a hint of disrespect towards Calita.

"You hate me this much?" She tilted her head and studied him, likely looking for weaknesses.

She would find none. He hadn't loved her enough to hate her. It dawned on him that there had been nothing between him and Miranda but lust and the fervor of a joined cause. Simon had married her against both his father's and his bear's wishes, scoffing at even the hint of destiny and soul mates. Looking back, he couldn't believe how wrong he'd been.

"I don't hate you." Simon's voice was firm.

Her leaving had stung his pride, but their failed marriage had been quickly pushed aside as he mourned the loss of his father. His new responsibilities hadn't allowed him the time to wallow over their divorce. He'd been busy building his father's failing farm into one of the most popular dude ranches on the east coast, bringing in money to their clan and stabilizing it. He'd spent every hour awake fighting to show the clan that he could be alpha and lead them and it paid off.

So many realizations rained on him as he stared down at his ex-wife, reminded of the battles they'd waged in the name of all shifters. He'd thought for the longest time that fighting was the only way to show strength. Coming back home, he'd learned the strength it took to stay and hold on to what his family had spent centuries building.

He'd not given his father enough credit for that.

"I've worked to build a good life here for my bears. I don't want you coming to disrupt it." He said quietly.

She blanketed the scheme ruminating behind her gaze and gave him innocent eyes. "I only came here for refuge."

The lie fell between them, the stench of it curling his lip. Miranda spoke as though he'd not fought beside her for years. As though he'd not helped her recruit shifters to their cause.

"You need to leave."

He couldn't make her leave the town, there were laws in place for that. Another way the government suffocated shifters, stifling protocols and traditions they'd self-governed with for centuries. But, he could kick her off his property. He walked away from her and gathered his horse from the corral where he'd left him. He cooed at the animal as he worked his saddle back onto the horse.

"What happened to you? You used to brawl with the best of us," she sneered, trailing behind him.

He still brawled, just in a different way. He now battled in a way people like Miranda would never acknowledge. Using the same fire he'd used on the front lines of the shifter war, he fought for his clan at home. For every inch the local government gave, he took a mile, or rather an acre. Five years later he'd had three hundred acres added to his ranch, and a steady stream of tourists. By the time the United States had abolished the Sanctuary restrictions, he'd turned the dying town of Bear Ridge into a thriving small city with no need for the government's help or interest in their intervention.

Simon had no doubt Miranda had an agenda in coming back to town. She would go away when she realized there was nothing here for her.

"I'm done with this conversation." He said with finality.

Putting her out of his mind, Simon swung back up on his horse and went back to work.

***

Calita cursed as she dropped the second pepper she was attempting to stuff. Simon's offer was playing in her head, throwing off her concentration.

Damn him.

There was no way she could dismiss him. When he proposed what he did, she'd been floored. One, by his audacity and two, by the fact that he seemed to want her. Her self-esteem had taken a beating along with her physical body when she'd been with David. Getting it back was a long, arduous road. The way Simon looked at her, the heat in his eyes was shocking, and flattering. His offer was insulting, and she admitted reluctantly, intriguing. She should have slapped his face for suggesting she would go along with an affair, but the idea of controlling it…

God that made her hot.

Control was something she longed for, in every aspect of her life. It would be a heady experience, controlling someone as powerful as Simon. It spoke on his self-confidence that he would offer that control so freely. Strangely, that pushed away some of her fear. She could sense he would be demanding during sex. He was the Alpha of this town so, hell yeah, he would be demanding, but instead of worry, need filled her. Her body heated, and a blush warmed her cheeks. She'd thought about him all night, dreamed about it even. She fanned her face, oh boy what dreams she'd had about him. The man was sexy and her imagination had no problem filling in details of what it would be like to be with him. By the time she'd finally got to sleep, it seemed like she was due to come down to work.

"Cali, table six wants to meet the chef," one of the waitresses announced as she grabbed her orders from the window.

"I don't have time, Amanda, please give them my apologies," Cali said, moving to the next task.

It wasn't the first time someone had asked to speak to her since she'd moved to town. She'd thought working for humans was demanding. Bears…she blew out a breath. They were demanding in a whole different way. Some were nosy, others, wanted to tell the chef directly how they wanted their dish cooked.

She snorted.

After the third person Selena cursed out on her behalf, she'd not had to worry about that kind of request again. Although, they were demanding, it was fun cooking for the bears. They loved their fresh fruits and vegetables, and she enjoyed creating and experimenting with vegetarian dishes. She'd been shocked to learn that they didn't eat as much meat as she imagined. Fresh fish and fresh produce were staples in Selena's restaurant. Along with pastries, man did those bears have a sweet tooth.

She loved cooking, but baking was her ultimate passion and making desserts for the bears made her genuinely happy. She was getting every penny's worth of her culinary training. She flinched, thinking of some of the disdain her ex had for her baking.

She would not think about David.

"Cali, a note from table six," Amanda dropped it on the window with a smirk and twirled off. Frowning, Cali picked it up.

Just saying hello. I've had a bad day. Come cheer me up?
-S-

Cali hissed as a wave of desire sped up her heart. The note was innocent, nothing sexual, but she couldn't suppress the shiver of awareness. She frowned, he had a bad day? She wondered if it was a ploy. She couldn't imagine a man as strong as Simon letting a bad day upset him. Tucking the note into her apron pocket she went back to cooking. Twenty minutes later, she couldn't get the note out of her mind. Curiosity wouldn't let her concentrate. Compulsion not easily explained urged her to go to him. She wanted to see him. Sighing, she washed her hands and gave up.

She grabbed two slices of lemon honey cake and walked out towards the front of the diner. She knew the cake was one of Simon's favorite. It had only taken a few well-placed questions and some teasing from the bears in the kitchen to find that out. He had a bad day, she told herself, and bringing him cake meant nothing.

He was at table six like Amanda said, tucked into one of the turquoise high–backed booths towards the far end of the diner. It was early into the dinner rush, so the place was not yet packed, even though the regulars had filled their favorite spots along the bar. Calita had only eyes for Simon, taking the time to study him. His shoulders were wide, the muscles beneath the polo shirt he wore, easy to discern. His chiseled features were serious; a small frown tilted his sensual mouth down, lines of exhaustion evident on his face. He'd pulled his long hair back from his face, into a bun towards the middle of his head, and good Lord, the man was fine. As though he could sense her gaze, his head raised and his dark eyes speared her. The exhaustion she saw moments ago was washed away as desire lit his eyes. Her heart fluttered. What woman wouldn't want all that attention focused on her?

He stood as she neared his table and grabbed the plates from her hands. He set them down on the table and turned to her, holding out his hands. She grabbed them, wanting to touch him, lifting her cheek. He bussed a small kiss across her skin, and took a deep breath.

She examined how she felt so close to him, and found that she wasn't uncomfortable, which, quite frankly surprised her. Her instincts weren't screaming, and she wasn't afraid for her safety with him. That said a lot. It was one of the reasons she found herself seriously considering his offer.

His eyes heated the longer they held hands and silence stretched between them. That same silence was shared by the rest of the diner. Calita looked around at the sudden stillness and caught several patrons' rapt attention on them.

Simon cleared his throat. "Thank you for coming to see me." He waited on her to sit.

Chatter resumed around them, as Calita slid onto the cushioned bench across from where his drink sat. "I only have a few minutes."

"You brought my favorite," he said smiling.

"I heard you had a bad day." She returned his smile.

His eyes heated, their color changing, darkening even more. Did that mean his bear was close? She was curious. She'd researched the hell out of shifters before she agreed to move to the town, but had never seen a shifter up close until she came to this town. They were across the country and in Chicago she was sure, but she hadn't known any. Shifters had been segregated and forced onto Sanctuaries towards this part of the country, so shifter populations were more concentrated in Southern cities. Towns like Bear Ridge were spread across the south.

Calita's gaze skimmed Simon's face in frank interest. What in the world could he want from her? From the tales about them, they could sense fear and according to Selena's husband, the sheriff, her aura fairly reeked of it. What could the alpha of the local shifters want with her?

"It's better now, how was your day?"

"It was good, tell me about your bad day." She did better letting people talk about themselves. Especially in this town when her every emotion was easily picked up by their other senses.

"Well, my ex-wife came by today." He dug into his dessert

"Ex-wife, I thought shifters only mated once?" Confusion bunched her brows.

"I made a lot of stupid mistakes in my youth. I married a woman my bear knew could not be my mate. I didn't quite believe in mates at the time." His eyes speared her.

A shiver of awareness worked down her spine and tightened her womb. God, but this man was direct. How a woman would be stupid enough to let him go, she'd never know.

"Does she do that often?" Calita asked, steering back to the subject to break the spell his eyes were putting her under.

"Come by? No, I haven't seen her in five years." Simon answered.

"What did she do that made your day bad?" she wondered what the ex-wife wanted, but would bite her tongue before asking.

She didn't know Simon well, but what she had heard about him told her he wouldn't proposition her if he and his ex-wife still had something going on. She would stay out of his business. Besides, he'd said no strings attached. Getting all personal would certainly add strings to their relationship…well, almost relationship. She wasn't sure if she would take him up on his offer.

"The fact that Miranda is in town does that. She says one thing, but likely wants something different." Simon sighed.

"What could she want from you?" *How's that for staying out of his business?* She silently berated herself. "I'm sorry, I didn't mean to pry."

"We used to be a part of the shifter rebellion. The peace we have with the humans is new and not something most of our group necessarily agreed with. More than likely she wants money to fund them. I can't imagine her asking me to join the fight again." Simon pushed his empty dessert plate from him.

"Are you curious at all about it?"

She couldn't believe she was asking such personal questions. They were crowding out of her mouth before she could filter. She wanted to ask so many more. She'd seen news reports of the shifter rebellion and their skirmishes with supremacists. Had he fought alongside them? Those weren't questions one asked when having a no-strings relationship, so instead, she squelched her curiosity.

Simon reached over and cut a piece of her cake with his fork. "I thought about it for about twenty minutes. It took that long for me to reign in my temper. But then I decided I didn't want to know." He held the fork in front of her lips.

She dropped her mouth open without thought, sighing as the lemon exploded on her tongue. She lifted her lids and caught him watching her mouth. His eyes had gone golden, a feral hunger filling them. His need was there for anyone to read.

She swallowed. "I'm sorry she ruined your day." Calita pushed her plate to him in offering.

Simon rewarded her with a big smile that caused a shaft of heat to surge through her. "How was your day, really?"

She thought about the nightmares she'd been having recently. "Good."

He raised an eyebrow and pointed his fork at her. "Tut-tut, tell me the truth."

"Not bad," she held up her hands. "Honestly, just had a little trouble sleeping, as usual. I love my job, and I love it here, so any time I'm in the kitchen my day is going well."

"You like it here?"

"Love it, it's a great town, Simon. You're a good alpha from what the bears around here have to say."

His eyes softened at the compliment. "Thank you."

She nodded and cleared her throat. If she wasn't careful, the man would totally worm his way into her heart. That would be the ultimate no-no for a no strings relationship. She stood and gathered their empty plates. "I need to get back to work."

He grabbed her hand and placed it between his, the warmth seeping into her skin. "Have you thought about my offer?"

Calita's heart raced. "As if I could think about anything else."

He smiled. The arrogance in the tilt of his lips made her legs weak. He didn't say anything else.

"I don't know yet," she said, rushing to fill the silence. If he could be direct, she could give him the respect of being honest with him.

"That's fair. I'm in no rush." His eyes flickered gold, and his voice deepened. "That's a lie. But, I'll try for patience. You'll learn that bears are slow and meticulous in all things."

Her nipples pebbled and scraped against the lace of her bra. Lord, but this man had a way about him. She cleared her throat and took a sip of his water from the table. He licked his lips, watching her mouth, a low growl rumbling his chest.

"I should go." She managed to whisper.

He nodded, his expression intense, blazing. "Thank you for the cake, and the conversation."

She hightailed it back to the kitchen. If she could make it through the rest of the shift without thinking about him, it would be a small miracle. She slowed her gait as the hair on the back of her neck stood up. There were eyes on her. She took a discreet look around and her eyes met the furious ones of a woman she didn't know. Calita raised her eyebrow, while she may be wary of men, she'd knock a bitch on her ass before she let herself be intimidated. She'd had no issues with any of the other women in Bear Ridge, could this woman be Simon's ex-wife? She turned her back on the woman, dismissing her as soon as the doors swung shut behind her.

– 4 –

Hours later, coming out of the shower, Simon's proposition was still circling Calita's mind. He was a tempting man. He didn't push, yet…somehow she knew he would give her but so long to make her decision. She sat on edge of the queen sized bed in her towel, applying lotion to her legs, wondering, not for the first time, why she even entertained his offer.

As she rubbed in the fragrant cream, she had to admit it was intriguing. That in and of itself was a good sign. Hormones she'd feared would lay forever dormant were flaring awake, all brought on by Simon's offer. For three years her body had felt encased in ice. It felt good to have it finally come alive. Simon's eyes made her body promises that she ached to explore. Was she ready for that?

The phone next to her bed started ringing and she glanced at the time with a frown. It was well after midnight. Who would call her this late?

"I don't know if my ego can take this, Calita." Simon's deep voice teased her over the line.

She took a shuddering breath, her body warming. Well, that didn't take long. She put the phone on speaker and walked over to the dresser drawers to get her clothes. "Do you have any idea what time it is?"

"I'm having a hard time sleeping." His voice deepened. "I thought perhaps you could talk to me and help me sleep."

She pulled on a pair of silk panties and smiled. "I don't know, Simon. That sounds intimate, and an awful lot like strings." She said sliding on a tank top.

His seductive chuckle sent a wave of arousal through her body. "Maybe if you talk dirty to me it will still fit within my offer."

She groaned. "I don't know if I can do what you want, Simon."

He hummed.

"I mean, I'm not the kind of person that can sleep with someone without emotions."

Right? She'd never been the kind of person that enjoyed sex either way, so an affair wasn't something she thought she'd ever be contemplating. She walked back to the bed and picked up the phone, leaning back against the padded headboard.

"You're completely cutting men from your life?" Simon's voice cut into her thoughts.

Calita sighed. "It's just not a good time for men in my life."

"That sounds like excuses. You forget I can tell what you're feeling, so I know you want me. It seems you're afraid to go after what you want."

She scoffed. "You don't know me, and I'm a grownup. My body doesn't control me."

"Now, that's a shame. Especially since I saw how flushed you got, and the way your breath shortened when I touched you." He sighed, a lustful sigh. "I know you want me." His voice lowered, the rumble sending pulses to her center. "I dare you to go after what you want, Calita."

Cali cursed his arrogance, and the truth of his words. "This isn't high school, Simon, I'm not going to sleep with you because you dare me," she sputtered.

He chuckled and her cursed body betrayed her. Moisture gathered between her legs.

"I dare you, Calita," he taunted, his voice even lower, drawing her nipples to tight points. "I can be to your room in twenty minutes, I can be inside you in thirty."

Cali barely suppressed a moan. "This is not a good idea, Simon," her voice was husky, arousal threaded throughout.

"I think it's a great idea. Say yes," his voice was snatching away her common sense.

"No."

"That didn't sound convincing at all, are you wet Cali?"

"Is this you allowing me to set the pace?" She said instead. No way would she tell him something so personal.

"Touch yourself for me, Cali," Simon cajoled, ignoring her question.

Her hands made the journey south before she even registered the movement.

"Twenty minutes, baby."

Cali shook her head. She knew how far outside of town his ranch was, no way he was making that drive without breaking several speed limits. Her hands slid into her panties, touching the lips of her sex. If she could just stop the throbbing… Why should she deny herself?

"Simon." It was neither a yes, nor a no.

"I dare you to say yes, Calita."

She shuddered as her finger brushed over her clit. Why was she saying no again? "Yes," she whispered.

"I'm already out the door," he rumbled.

Calita stared at the phone with a sense of disbelief. He had hung up on her and by his word was on his way over to the small hotel adjacent to the diner where she was staying. It took her all of about a minute to register that, before she scrambled off her bed. She ran to the restroom and yanked the scarf from her head and brushed her hair back until it gleamed, debating whether or not to leave it loose or pull it into a ponytail. She cursed herself ten minutes later as she tossed clothes around, trying to figure out what to wear. True to his word, a little over twenty minutes later Simon knocked softly on her door.

She opened the door and he stood there looking impossibly handsome in a pair of jeans molded to his thighs and a loose white t-shirt. A dark citrus scent wafted from him, his own hair wet as though he himself had just stepped from the shower. The scuffed boots on his feet just reinforced his rugged look and her breasts tingled and swelled in anticipation. A delicious ache invaded her body, reminding her of how long it had been since she'd had sex.

This was crazy.

She shouldn't let this man into her room. He would play hell with her heart. Even knowing that, she stepped back and allowed him entrance.

Simon stared at her instead of coming in and grabbed her waist, pulling her closer. She peered down the hallway to be sure no one saw them. His warm hands burned through the thin material of the tank top she wore. He kissed her and her brain scrambled. Her knees went weak and her arms went up to his shoulders to brace herself. Simon walked her into the room, not breaking the kiss and shut the door with his foot.

Calita barely suppressed a moan as his hands roamed under her shirt. A jolt of electricity went through her everywhere he touched.

"Well, now, that's how you welcome a man." Simon smiled, arrogant from top of his head to soles of his scuffed boots.

She stepped back, breathless. The thought that, perhaps she was in over her head, popped up. "This isn't a good idea, Simon."

"I think it's a great idea, Calita." He leaned over and sucked on her neck.

All the reasons it was a bad idea flew from her mind. She moaned and arched her neck. His hand roamed under her tank top, caressing her back. The texture of his rough hands sent shivers across her skin. Calloused fingers brushed her stomach. Shyness had her holding his hands in place, keeping him from roaming too far up.

"Say yes, Cali," he whispered, pulling her ear into his mouth.

Her knees went weak, and he gripped her tighter. It raised her respect for him that he didn't assume because he was there, he would get sex.

"It'll be so good." He captured her lips, sipping from her mouth in sweet, drugging kisses.

God. She closed her eyes as the room spun. He cupped her breast, one finger caressing the nipple. He lifted her body and the cool wall against her back shocked her out of her stupor.

"Simon, wait." Her chest heaved as she fought for breath, fought to get the desire under control.

He wrapped her leg around his waist and inserted his hips between her legs.

Sweet Mercy.

The feel of him at her center stole her breath. Moisture gathered, dampened her shorts, and her clit swelled, throbbed. He moved, lifted his hips, rubbing his erection against the nub once, twice. She closed her eyes and fought the orgasm starting to build.

"Do you really want me to wait?" He trailed kisses across her collarbone, skimming his fingers along her inner thigh.

She shook her head. No, she didn't want to wait. She wanted him. God, she wanted him with a fervor that pushed all good sense aside.

"Say it aloud, baby. Tell me you want this so there's no misunderstanding," he coaxed, his hips grinding into hers.

She whimpered. Heat pooled low in her abdomen.

He chuckled. "Do you want me to stop, Cali?"

"No." It came out in a hoarse whisper. She cleared her throat. "I want you."

"Good girl." He kissed her.

More to say he devoured her.

His tongue pushed into her mouth and consumed her, stealing her control, her reasoning. Calita moaned and raised her hips, grinding into his erection.

He growled low in his throat. "Oh, Cali, the things I'm going to do this gorgeous body."

His words sent fire through her blood.

Cali panted as he kissed the tops of her breast. Her nipples strained against the front the shirt. He leaned over and pulled one into his mouth, t-shirt and all. Her back bowed. He hollowed his cheeks, pulling her breast in further.

He stopped, she moaned.

"Take off your shirt if you don't want it ripped."

His words penetrated her fog of arousal. A moment of self-consciousness wriggled into her mind as she thought about exposing her scars. Instead of lifting her shirt, she pulled the collar down under her breasts. His belt buckle clanged as he struggled to take off his own clothes. Her mouth went dry as he pulled down his jeans. His thick, muscular thighs bunched as he pushed his pants down. His erection, thick and dark, stood straight and her breath seized in hunger.

"Damn it." His jeans stopped at the boots he forgot to take off.

A giggle escaped as he fought to take both boots and pants off. She smothered another laugh as he stumbled. He gave her a stern look and her shoulders shook with laughter. His trouble loosened more of the tension in her. He finally wrestled the pants off and stalked to her.

"You're not supposed to laugh at me, woman." His lips twitched and he reached into his jeans pocket before tossing his clothes over his shoulder. "I'm the big, strong alpha, you're supposed to be awed by my body."

She giggled, "I am very much in awe of your body."

He lifted her as though she weighed nothing, and she squealed in surprised. Lust had her mind fogged, she hadn't even considered the strength of a bear. It was another thing going on the plus column, right along with the cock brushing against her stomach as Simon easily carried her to the bed. Moisture gathered between her legs in anticipation.

"Now, where was I?" He murmured, staring down at her body, sheathing his cock with a condom.

"You said something about doing things to my body," she whispered, arching her back.

His growl moved through her body like fire and he hovered over top of her. He kissed her, his hands gliding down her legs. He gasped into her mouth when he realized she wasn't wearing underwear. His eyes went darker, a feral, hungry look suffusing his face. He backed up and a smile tilted up his lips. His dark eyes glowed gold and a purr rumbled his chest. He pulled down her loose shorts and kissed her hip bone, taking a deep breath once the shorts were down around her ankles.

The long lick of his tongue to her center sent her hips airborne. She grabbed his hair and held him in place as he ate her. His tongue danced across her sex, dipping and tasting her. His fingers were no less busy, driving in and out of in slow strokes. Calita threw her head back and her legs wider, giving him better access. Simon wasted no time taking advantage. His tongue swept across her clit, before he sucked it into his mouth.

She didn't want him to stop, but she also wanted to feel him inside her. She pulled his head from her sex.

"Inside, now," she ordered.

He growled, giving one last lick to her center before crawling over her body. "I need you to understand this first time I plan to take my time. I've wanted to be inside of you from my first sight of you."

"There is nothing holding us back." She whispered. He went to lift her shirt and she tensed and bat at his hands. "Need you," she breathed out to distract him.

He fit himself between her legs. She locked them around his waist, anxious to have him. She expected some kind of panic to set in, but her head was full of Simon. His scent wrapped around her, making her dizzy. His weight on her made her feel secure. She closed her eyes and savored the feel of his firm, soft skin beneath her palms. He nuzzled into her neck and she breathed out, her chest expanding and the warm feeling of belonging suffused her. Her breath hitched when he circled her entrance with his erection. He brought his head up and kissed her.

He rubbed his face against the side of hers. "You ready for me?"

She opened her eyes when he paused.

"There you are," he whispered. "You here with me?"

"Yes," she whispered. "I want you."

His chest rumbled with a purr that clenched her womb. He pushed in slowly stretching her channel, rocking slowly back and forth to give her body time to loosen. Each time making it easier for him to go deeper on the next stroke. Liquid flooded her center, easing the way with his every push. She squeezed her eyes shut, her breath catching as the muscles of her sex flexed around his cock. She opened her eyes and was speared by his hungry gaze. It was open, vulnerable and her heart clenched. His look was deeper than just sex. She lifted her hips, wanting every bit of him.

He leaned over and nipped her lips. "You feel amazing."

She smiled, her body relaxing more under his expert touch.

"More, Cali."

The soft-spoken command sped her heart rate. His hips drove into her as she scraped her nails across his back.

"Shit, woman," he whispered across her lips.

He grabbed under her knee, lifting her leg higher. His strokes deepened, hitting over that spot deep inside her. Tingles started at the base of her spine and she moved her hips to urge him faster.

He chuckled at her intent. "Ah-ah, I plan to enjoy every second inside your body."

"Simon," she hissed when he hit that spot again.

"Yes, baby?"

She wanted to beg him. The top of his groin brushed across her clit and she gasped. He smiled, the self-satisfied smile of a man who knew what he was doing. She clenched her sex and he sucked in a breath, his cocky smile dropping. His thrusts picked up speed. She squeezed again, arching her back.

"Calita," his desperate whisper brushed the skin of her neck.

The hair on her arms raised as electricity traveled the length of her body. He gripped her hips, holding her down as he drove into her. His face a mask of concentration, he fucked her as though he had all the time in the world. She savored every minute, luxuriating in the sensation. It had been years since she'd allowed a man this close to her. Simon was worth the wait. He played her body like an instrument he'd spent years perfecting.

Her abdomen clenched tight, an orgasm building. The muscles in her legs tightened as she fought to reach it.

***

Calita's hips bucked in his hands, her legs tightening around his waist as she worked towards her orgasm. He sucked the skin of her neck into his mouth, wanting desperately to bite down and seal her to him. Her mewl sounded in his ear and tender feelings he wasn't expecting just yet clenched his heart. Her wet sex surrounded his shaft, pulling at his sanity and control.

Fuck, this woman was everything.

He sped his strokes, his own orgasm barreling towards him. Power from his bear flooded his body and surrounded his mate, the animal leaving its mark on Calita, though they wouldn't be able to claim her yet.

"Simon," she panted.

"A little longer, baby, stay with me a little longer," he begged, closing his eyes, fighting to stave off the orgasm nearly overtaking him.

He slowed his strokes, angling his hips until he hit…

Her mouth opened, her long moan filling the room.

Yeah, that was the reaction he wanted.

"Please," she gasped.

He couldn't deny her the softly spoken plea. He traced her face with his gaze, cataloguing every change in her expression. He leaned down and captured her lips, his tongue spearing into her mouth as lights danced on the edge of his vision. He couldn't hold back any longer. She moaned into his mouth, her sex pulsing, squeezing around his shaft as she came. Her orgasm dragged him under, his body bowing with the sensations flooding his body. From the tip of his toes, up to his scalp, nerve endings flared alive. His hips jerked as Calita's sex clenched tightly around him, each throb dragging his orgasm longer.

Shit.

He was going to bite her.

He grit his teeth, and tightened one arm around her body, burying his head into the crook of her neck. The other arm dug into the mattress, claws exploding from his hands. He pleaded, bargaining with his bear to let their mate have time. She would come to them. The growl that built in his chest showed his other half's disgruntled attitude. His hips jerked, an aftershock sending tingles throughout his body. She moaned beneath him, her body finally going limp as he wrung the last of her orgasm from her.

He fought to get his breath back, rolling over to his side, pulling her with him, not daring to leave the warmth of Calita's body. His chest heaved with deep breaths as his heart beat tumbled through his chest. Her heavy exhalations heated the side of his neck. He sighed and cuddled into her side, still hard inside her. He lifted her chin and kissed her, their tongues tracing each other's in a lazy rhythm. She pulled back and kissed his chin, snuggling into him. They laid quiet that way for a few minutes, Calita tracing slow circles around his chest.

He rubbed his chin along the top of her hair. "If you're trying to talk me into round two, I promise you, that's the way to do it."

She sighed.

"What's wrong?"

"I don't think I can do this, Simon."

He wouldn't panic. At least not yet. He gently pulled from her body, discarding the condom in the trash can next to her bed. He turned and angled to see her face. "Tell me your fears, Calita, perhaps I can alleviate some of your stress."

She avoided his gaze. "This isn't me. I don't do no string relationships. I can't separate my body from my feelings."

"And if I want your feelings?" Simon tilted her chin towards him and held his breath for her answer.

She closed her eyes. "I'm not fit to be anything you need."

"How do you know what my needs are, baby?"

"Shifters have two modes, one-night stands or mating, I can't be your mate."

He released her chin and propped up his head to get a better look at her. "And you know shifters' sexual habits how?" His voice had gone deep as jealousy aroused his bear.

"I read about it." She looked away.

"So, you're basing what we could have, to what, an article you read?"

She blew out an impatient breath. "That's not what I meant."

"What would you do if I told you, you were my mate?"

He trailed his fingers down the side of her body, pushing beneath the t-shirt she still wore. His cock twitched, the feel of her soft skin rousing a body part that would be useless for at least another few minutes. There was plenty that could be done until his dick decided it was ready for round two, though. He licked his lips in anticipation.

She sighed, putting a hand to his forehead as he dipped to lick at her collar. "I don't know that I'm ready for that."

Round two or the mating? His bear didn't much care to clarify, wanting another taste of her. Simon pushed down the V of her t-shirt, hoping to free a nipple.

"Simon," Calita growled. "Focus."

He shook the lust clear and fought to concentrate on his mate. *What were they talking about again? Oh...yeah...*

"What if I amended my earlier offer to you?"

Her body stiffened. "In what way?"

"Same offer, complete control to you, but instead of no strings, you give me time to convince you that we belong together."

"That's…" She paused and studied his face. "Belong together? That's a huge step past no strings attached."

He pulled her hand up and kissed her fingertips. "I'm not letting you go, Calita."

Her heart sped up and the acrid smell of fear permeated the air. Her eyes widened and she jerked back, her body stiffening as she rolled onto her back.

"I don't mean…calm down, baby. I simply meant, I don't want to give up what we could have." He rolled over her and braced his hands on either side of her face. It took only a millisecond to realize that caging her in was a wrong move. Panic had her eyes wide and her scent sharp with anxiety. His bear whined in response.

He sat up, bringing her with him. "Breathe with me, Cali." He pulled her gaze to his eyes, and breathed deep, soon she was breathing with him, their heartbeats matching as was right for his mate. His bear's magic wrapped around her, settling her further.

"When I told you I would give you control, I meant it. You're the only person on this planet who has total control over me. I'm sorry if I rushed this, I got a little worked up thinking about you." He studied her eyes, and saw the moment she realized what he said.

"I don't know, Simon."

"I'm not asking you for anything other than what we talked about. Remember?" He rubbed his cheek in the crook of her neck, marking her with his scent to hopefully calm her.

"Yes," she whispered.

He kissed her, this time plunging his tongue into her mouth to get one final taste of her before he left. "I'm going to go, let you rest. Give you back your safe space, yes?"

Tears shone in her eyes as she nodded.

"I'm sorry if I scared you."

"It's okay," she whispered.

"Will you call me when you wake tomorrow?" He glanced at the clock next to her bed, "well…rather later this afternoon when you wake."

Her head jerked in agreement.

"Promise?" he whispered against her lips.

"Promise."

He kissed her tenderly, careful to reign in his bear. Last thing he wanted to do was scare their mate more. "I'm willing to wait until you're ready, Calita. I'll try for more patience." He brushed the tear from her face and kissed her cheek.

He lay next to her for several heartbeats until she completely calmed. Once her heart slowed, he nuzzled against her cheek and rolled out of bed.

Getting dressed, he left her room quickly before he gave in to the urge to stay. He was familiar with the panic attack she'd gone through. He recognized the signs of PTSD. He'd seen it enough times throughout his old life to understand. He'd also seen it in some of the bears when he'd taken over from his father. Before they'd had their rights recognized by the government, humans had taken their fear and anger out on any shifter they'd managed to corner. In his old life, he'd been a part of the shifters they'd called to enact justice. In this new life as Alpha, he'd had to learn how to take care of his bears in the aftermath. Five years as alpha and it was a change he was still getting used to, but he was grateful for the experience because now he could help his mate.

He first needed to find out what happened to her.

He went downstairs, unlocking and starting his truck from the entrance of the hotel. When he got in, he pulled out his cellphone.

Nate answered on the first ring, his voice sleepy. "Alpha."

"Nate, I want you to look into Calita."

"In what way?" More alert, the sheriff shuffled around, murmuring to his mate to go back to sleep.

"I want to know everything about her, and why she came to this town. Everything." It was something he should've done once his bear recognized her as his mate, but he'd wanted to get to know her the old-fashioned way. Now he was doubting that decision.

Nate was quiet on the other end, and for a moment, Simon assumed his phone had cut out. "Nate?"

"Yeah, I'm here. I'll find out what I can."

"I want everything, Nate." He didn't feel bad about the power he put behind the request.

"Yes, Alpha." Nate ended the call.

Simon buckled his seatbelt and put his car in gear. Nate was nothing if not efficient. It was only a matter of time before the sheriff would have something on Calita. Hopefully something that would help him figure out a way to help her.

$$-\;5\;-$$

Up early again, Calita had taken her car into the neighboring town for some shopping. She needed space from Bear Ridge, and its Alpha to think. Last night with Simon had been…she sighed. The sex had been amazing, and that was different for her. Her body was pleasantly sore. Her cheeks burned as she thought about having to call down to housekeeping for new sheets. She threw away the other ones when she left the hotel, no way was she explaining the claw marks scoring the fabric. If she was really smart, Calita would still be in bed, basking in her after glow. She'd not had a lot of sexual partners, partly due to her awkwardness around the opposite sex. It had made her ripe for the picking where David was concerned.

He'd charmed her, lulled her into dropping her friends and focusing all her energy on him. She shook her head and remembered her therapist's words. She wasn't the only woman who'd been in a domestic situation. She had to forgive herself, and remember that she'd finally been strong enough to leave. She had to quit dwelling on the past and focus on her future.

Last night with Simon had gone a long way towards making her think about the future. The way he'd handled her panic attack was nothing short of amazing to her. She needed clarity. She knew just where to go for that. Calita pulled into downtown Bear Ridge and parked her car a little way down from her destination. Anika's shop was the perfect place to go for something to help her relax. She walked past the bookstore and made a note to stop on her way back. She waved as she got to the real estate office and the lone woman who occupied it. She started to pass, but stopped. She'd been in town a year now. Wasn't it time for her to find a place of her own?

"Calita, hi," Jerica greeted. Wearing a simple dark green sheath, with a black blazer on top, the no-nonsense woman stood as she entered.

She'd slowly learned the names of the locals as they came into the diner. Jerica, in particular, always came in on Sunday afternoons for a pie for her Sunday dinner. Apple, nothing fancy, she'd always say.

Calita smiled. "Hi, Jerica. I wanted to come in and get some listings. I think it's time for me to look for an apartment."

Jerica frowned. "I thought you and the alpha…" She paused and shook her head. "I'm sorry that's not my business." She walked back to her desk and opened one of her drawers, handing Cali a few brochures. "Now, if you're talking in town, there are a couple of cottages not too far from Selena's diner. If you want something with more amenities, you'll have to go the next town over. Pleasant Mills is slightly bigger than Bear Ridge, of course, so they're a couple of small apartment buildings with vacancies."

"I just came from Pleasant Mills, that's not too bad of a drive," she murmured, more to herself.

"Look it over and let me know what you decide," Jerica said.

"Thanks so much, I will." Cali stuffed the listings into her purse and waved goodbye.

She passed the town's only hair salon, and not even the smell of chemicals could mask the aromas coming from Anika's store two doors down. Anika had the best candles she'd ever had the pleasure of using. She carried other things, lotions, all-natural shampoos and soaps that made Calita a frequent visitor to the shop.

A small tinkle announced her arrival. Anika looked up from where she was mixing at the counter. She was Native American, Chickasaw to be exact, as was a good portion of the town from what she'd observed. Anika's long, wavy black hair, was loose, and flowing down to the middle of her back. Her skin was bronze, her eyes dark and wide, as she looked up and spotted Calita. She gave her a warm smile and waved her in. Calita remembered when she'd first discovered the shop. Anika had taken one look at her and went around the shop gathering candles and bath salts. She'd told Cali she would find a measure of peace with her move and had she wished her luck. So far, she had been right.

"Good morning, Anika," Cali greeted her.

Anika's brows bunch and she tilted her head.

"What?" Cali pat the top of her head, making sure her hair was in place.

"I don't know." Anika pursed her lips and tapped her chin. "You're lighter, but not. What's going on?"

Cali blushed. "I came for more candles. For the most part, they've been helping me sleep."

Anika nodded. "I knew they would." She walked over to the shelf where she stored her candles and reached for the ones she'd given Cali earlier, she also pulled down another candle. "Use this one as well, just when you're sitting around relaxing. This will clear your mind and help you make those decisions you're struggling with."

Calita blew out a breath. "How did you…"

Anika shrugged, then sniffed the air. "Oh, I see." A smirk pushed up her lips.

"What now?" Cali groaned.

"Nothing." Anika pretended to zip her lips. "Anything else you wanted?"

"Well, I have the day off, so I'm just going to drift in here and smell everything."

"Feel free."

Calita smiled at Anika's laugh. She wandered aimlessly down the aisles, her fingers drifting across the different items sold. Her steps were slow as she passed the soap display, the bars in coordinating hues drawing her eye. She didn't need any more soap at the moment, but the smells were tempting.

Her mind went to Simon and what he would like. She debated asking Anika, but she had a feeling it would only make the woman tease her outright.

Her thoughts drifted to what he'd said last night. She wondered what he meant by her being his mate, and if he was serious. He'd already been married, against his bear's wishes according to him and the gossip mill in town, maybe he didn't know his own mind. Could she trust his words? She jerked to attention as she heard an inhuman scream.

"Oh no." Anika's harsh whisper reached her down the aisle. "Oh no."

Calita turned and searched outside the window of the shop and noticed a young kid in the middle of the square, his body hunched over, his face etched in pain. Fur rippled up and down his arms as he screamed again. She raced out to help him, unable to take the pain transforming his face. People gathering yelled at her to stop. She didn't understand what was happening, but the kid was in pain and she refused to stand by and watch. She touched his shoulder and he growled. Her heart leaped in her chest, its rapid drumbeat matching the kids. She squelched it, a pro at hiding her feelings these past few years. It served her well in a town full of shifters with extraordinary senses.

"What's wrong, how can I help?" Her voice only barely wavered. Kudos to her, considering she was scared out of her mind.

"I don't know," he croaked. "It hurts, my bear wants out. Oh God!"

Her stomach surged, and bile rose as she realized the kid was going to turn into a bear, right in the middle of the town square. Hell, right in front of her! She'd read up on bears and shifters before she made the decision to take Selena up on her offer of a job and she was pretty sure there was a protocol for them shifting in public. Especially in a place where tourists and humans frequented. Not only was the kid in pain, but he could be in a world of trouble with the law. No, she wouldn't let that happen to him.

She'd read that the younger bears had a harder time with their instincts, and from the panic widening this kid's eyes, she had to guess it was his first time shifting. How much control would he have? A fresh wave of fear threatened to eat through her calm façade.

She rubbed his arms. "Okay, okay. I don't think this is a good place to let him out. What can we do?"

He shook his head, his dark eyes wide, and glittering as he and bear struggled. Sweat beaded along the brown skin of his forehead. Not good. She took a deep breath.

Her mind flipped through techniques her therapist talked about to handle her own panic attacks. "Well, let's try breathing, yes?" Calita pushed out a breath through her lips and breathed in through her nose. "Follow me, okay."

He nodded. They breathed together for a few minutes until someone shouted out a warning from behind her. His attention diverted, claws pierced his hands and he screamed in pain.

She gripped his shoulders. "No, no, focus on me, focus on me. Let's breathe, we were doing so great. Tell me your name."

"Cole," he grit out.

Tears leaked from his eyes, and she hurt for him. She grabbed his cheeks and pulled his attention. They looked into each other's eyes and she started breathing again. Soon, he matched her rhythm. She rubbed a hand down his arm, her clammy palm cold in contrast to his scorching skin. His body temperature lowered as they continued their breaths, and his body relaxed, the fur slowly receding as the wild look left his eyes.

Collectively their heart beats slowed and he shuddered in relief. "Thank you." He whispered.

She nodded, unable to say anything as what she'd done came crashing around her. She could've been seriously hurt. What had she been thinking?

***

Simon was leaning against the wooden fence surrounding the corral where they trained the trail horses. His Beta, Gavin, was putting one of the new horses through its paces. They'd bought it at the last state auction, and so far he was satisfied with their purchase. His arms were crossed on the wooden post, the rough wood scraping against his forearms as he watched.

He heard the familiar engine growl of the sheriff's ancient jeep and frowned. Nate always came through, but Simon had just called him last night, hell, early morning, if he was being technical. No way had Nate been able to get information on Calita that quickly, unless he had it already. Though, his cousin could be stopping by about something else entirely. Nate became sheriff after their uncle had retired, and there wasn't much happening in town that he didn't know about and have a handle on. It could be any number of things Nate was visiting about.

Intrigued, Simon turned as the vehicle pulled to a stop a few yards away. Nate took his time unfolding his six foot six, massive frame out of the jeep, his slow gait normal for the male. The sheriff obviously hadn't started his shift yet. His shoulder length hair was loose around his face, still wet from his morning shower. His uniform shirt was open at his throat and tucked into a pair of worn denim jeans. Nate looked like their grandfather, from the sharp blade of his nose, to the angular chin, his face wide, serious.

Nate's feet shuffled in the sand as he moved to stand next to Simon. "*Chokma*, Alpha?"

"Doing fine, Sheriff. It's a little early in the day for you to be visiting. If you need something to do, your wife is running a gambling ring out of her restaurant."

Nate grunted. "That woman."

"How much did you lose?"

"Thirty dollars. You're getting slow in your old age, cousin."

Simon guffawed at Nate's disgruntled look. The laidback male had met his match in his mate. Selena's boisterous personality was the opposite of the stoic, quiet bear that was the sheriff. He'd grown up with Nate, and even as a cub, his cousin had been a serious creature. Though it didn't exactly translate into him staying out of trouble. Simon smiled in memory. Nate had a charm all his own that had talked them out of their fair share of punishments.

"I have the information you need."

Simon sucked in a breath of surprise. So he was right. "That was fast, even for you, Nate."

Nate shrugged. "You didn't seem inclined to wait."

"You have the right of it." Simon turned and nodded his head towards an empty pasture. "Walk with me."

They walked silently until they were well out of earshot of his Beta. A bear's hearing was one of their more powerful senses, so they'd walked nearly a hundred yards before they came to a stop.

"What did you find?"

Nate tucked his hands in his pockets and looked at Simon for a long moment before his dark eyes lowered in respect. "I debated whether to tell you. You're my alpha and so you understand how much respect I have for Calita to not come to you until I was sure."

Simon nodded in understanding. "She's my mate, Nathan. I wouldn't have asked you on a whim."

Nate sighed and rubbed his hands down his pants. "That's what I figured. You sure you don't want your mate to tell you herself?"

"That bad, huh?"

"It's mighty personal." Was his answer.

Simon sighed and ran a hand through his hair. "Well, shit. Is she in immediate danger?" He pushed down on his bear as he waited for the answer.

"Not that I can see. You'll be the first to know if that changes," Nate promised.

"Fine, I'll wait." His bear clawed against his chest, his muscles stretching with the need to get in his bear skin and track down their mate. It took a moment, but he wrestled the stubborn beast back under control.

"I'll let you get on with your day, cousin." Nate walked off.

"Nate." Simon stopped the sheriff's retreat. "At the first sign."

Nate nodded. "I swear, Alpha."

Simon stayed out in the pasture and took a moment to get his bearings. He wondered what Calita had gone through. She'd been hurt, that much he knew, and judging from Nate's reluctance to share, it must have been bad. His bear had already felt the pain of her soul, it was there in her eyes every time he'd gotten a look at her. With no small amount of arrogance, he knew he and his bear were the only ones who would heal Calita. He thought about the panic in her eyes last night when he'd told her he wouldn't let her go. That was fear, the kind of fear that made him wary. Made his bear want to take her to his den and keep her safe. He would wait on her to tell him, even if it took every bit of his patience.

"Simon!" Nate called to him from his jeep.

He looked up and jogged towards the sheriff, hearing the urgency in his voice. "What happened?"

"Trouble in town. Calita's involved." Nate jumped into his patrol vehicle.

Simon leapt into the passenger side and buckled in. Nate grabbed his radio and sped out, making a quick three-point turn.

"Report status," Nate ordered.

Static proceeded his deputy's answer. "Talia's boy is going through puberty early. He's transitioning right in the middle of downtown. We got reports that Calita's trying to talk him down."

Nate cursed. "I'm still twenty minutes out, who's there?"

"We sent Donovan, he's there now. Whatever Calita's doing is working, Don said he didn't want to interfere and spook them."

"Good call. Make sure he knows to step in at the first sign of him shifting," Nate ordered and slammed the radio down.

"Faster, Nate," Simon snapped.

"Trust me, I'm giving her everything."

He cursed his cousin's ancient jeep as it rattled, going barely over the posted speed limit. The department had brand new trucks, but Nate insisted on using the jeep their uncle had driven. Simon rode silently, his heart in his throat, his bear strangely calm. The creature was quite content that its mate was, probably subconsciously, stepping into her duty as alpha female. He had no such confidence. Calita had been through her own trauma, he couldn't imagine what a scared cub would do with her fear scenting the air.

The radio crackled a few minutes later. "Sheriff, we got it under control. Talia and Jim are there with the boy, and Calita is fine, over."

"Roger," Nate answered.

Their speed didn't slow and Simon was grateful. By the time they pulled up, the crowd was slowly dispersing and the boy was wrapped in a blanket in his parents' arms. His mate and Anika were bent with their heads together a few yards off. Simon jumped out of the truck before Nate could stop all the way. Talia broke off from her son and rushed to Calita. She grabbed his mate into a tight hug. Though she kept her face neutral, Calita's body language suggested she was uncomfortable with the sentiment. The mother gave her one last hug and went back to her family.

Simon walked up to Calita and grabbed her arm, marching her from the crowd. He kept his grip light, despite his fear. "Don't do something so incredibly stupid like that again."

Surprised by his tone, she flinched, snatching her arm from his grip. "It was handled, and never call me stupid."

Though she was doing an admirable job of squelching it, her fear scented the air around her. His bear swiped at his subconscious to calm down.

"I apologize for my tone, though I didn't call you stupid. I just…you can't approach a transitioning male. They don't have control over their bear yet. Especially a cub so young. You could've been seriously hurt. They don't know their strength. I was scared half to death when Nate got the call."

"I did, though. I approached a…a transitioning male, and I calmed him down. You're welcome." Her gaze raked his face with a scathing look before she walked away.

He stood stunned almost a full minute, her fire igniting his own. His bear growled in approval, before Simon rushed after her. She was standing next to her car door, her hands trembling as she grabbed her keys from her purse. He moved close until his body covered her back. Relief at feeling her curves against him made him shake.

"I'm sorry, you're right, you handled it well."

"Don't talk to me like that. Ever, Simon. I won't allow it." Her voice was soft, but strong.

"I swear." He also swore to himself he would get to the bottom of what made her so fearful and defensive. He kissed her neck. "Are you hurt at all?"

She nodded.

"Are you headed into work?"

She shook her head, but said nothing.

"Are you no longer speaking to me, darling?" He brushed a hand across her shoulder.

She shuddered and he caught sight of her reflection in the glass. She was crying. He turned her around, and used his thumb to wipe her tears. "I'm sorry, my love."

"It's not you...I was scared shitless, it's just left over adrenaline." She sniffled, shaking her head.

He pulled her into his arms and held her tight as she let out a shuddering breath.

"I need to get back." Her voice was muffled against his chest.

"Give me a few. Please, Calita." His need to reassure himself that she was safe had him trembling. He marked her cheek with his scent, and inhaled at the crook of her neck, allowing the feel of her safe in his arms to soothe him and hopefully her. He sighed. "I'll call you once I'm done dealing with this. Will you be okay driving home?"

She sighed and dabbed her eyes with the knuckles of her fingers. "It's right up the road, I'm not a child."

He pushed his nose into her neck. His bear rumbled out a purr using the vibrations to soothe their mate. Her arms finally wrapped around his waist and her body relaxed into his embrace.

"I'm not saying you are. You talked down a scared cub, and you've already admitted your adrenaline is high. You're likely to crash soon. I just want to make sure you arrive safely." He nipped her chin, before catching her gaze again. "Text me when you get home?"

She snorted and bumped her forehead against his shoulder.

"What?"

She looked up and kissed his cheek. "Nothing, you're sweet. Protective. I'm realizing the difference."

"From what?"

"Controlling," she said and got in her car.

She was cranked up and pulling out before he realized the implications of what she said. He watched her drive off, hands on his hips, wondering at the woman who was his mate.

"Alpha." Someone called his attention and he turned back to the scene.

Anika stood on the edge of the dissipating crowd. He inclined his head at his cousin before joining her.

"She'll make a good alpha female." Anika's soft words brought no small amount of pride to him.

Calita had talked down a skittish bear, taking care of the teenager in the way only an alpha female could. He wondered if she was even aware of the instinct.

He smiled. "Now I only have to convince her to accept that. No biggie, right?"

Anika snorted out a laugh, her hands shaking as she pushed back her hair. He moved closer to his cousin, wrapping her in a hug. Her bear reached for his, seeking comfort from its alpha. He rubbed her back a moment, giving her the touch she needed to calm herself.

She sighed. "Good luck, cousin. You'll need it. Calita is a little more independent than you're used to." She rubbed her cheek against his jaw and left him in the middle of the street.

He shook his head at the understatement and looked around. Tourists and townspeople alike milled about, their expressions varying between shock and excitement. He sighed, he wanted to go after his mate to make sure she really was ok but, he needed to reassure the humans and double check on the cub. The last thing he needed was for tourists to leave this town and spread stories of wild shifters who couldn't control their youth. Keeping the government's nose out of his town was his main focus as alpha. No one wanted another attempt at apartheid. It had barely worked the first time, nothing but war would result from a second attempt. He turned back and saw Miranda standing on the outside of the crowd with a male he didn't recognize. He sniffed the air.

Make that a bear he didn't recognize.

His beast growled. Already riled, aggressive energy raised the hair on his arms. He marched to them, ignoring his ex-wife.

"You stepped onto my territory without permission."

The male lowered his gaze in false submissiveness and Simon's bear amped up his power.

"I only arrived recently, Alpha, and was going to make myself known to you. I'm Charles Rossel."

Simon smelled his lies and his bear wanted him out of town. He narrowed his eyes. He couldn't quite kick him out without some sort of offense first, though. "Where are you from?"

"Atlanta. I came up with my mate, she talked about this place, and I've heard of how tight a ship you keep here."

"Is that right?" He gave Miranda a cursory glance, wandering exactly what she told the male to get him interested.

"If you have some time..."

"I don't. File the proper paperwork to request a meeting like everyone else before you." Simon cut off the male and gave him his back, letting Charles Rossel know he feared nothing from him.

He didn't want anything to do with Miranda or her schemes. Her scent from the other day made more sense now that he knew she was mated. Miranda had tried to hide that fact from him. Which led him to believe she wanted something more than safe harbor like she claimed. Whatever her goal was in coming back, she'd not succeed. He was done operating in the shadows, and there was no longer a place for her here. He'd have someone watch them while they were in town until Miranda, once again, became bored with country life and left.

- *6* -

Calita smiled and waved as Jeremiah pulled up to the back of Selena's restaurant. He was making their morning delivery of the current season of fruit and vegetables. The executive chef took care of these types of things, something she'd made clear to Selena she was not, but here she was early in the morning, waiting on produce delivery. She wouldn't complain about waking early, she'd barely slept last night.

Another nightmare, but this one plagued with transforming bears along with her ex-boyfriend. Nearly a week since she'd jumped in to help that kid and she was still dreaming of bears. She sighed. She'd talked to Simon every night since then, and she could admit that hearing his voice had helped. He kept his promise and didn't push her. Every night they talked for at least an hour, getting to know each other. He was sweet, funny in the driest way. Though he kept their conversations light for the most part, there were times when he reminded her that he'd not only been inside her body, but that she'd enjoyed it.

Once.

She'd slept with him once, yet her body craved him as though they'd been together for years. She smoothed a hand over her heated face. Simon had been explicit in detailing what he wanted to do with her body the next time he saw her. She pinched her t-shirt and shuffled it to fan her body. She would call him. Why deny herself? The mate part did make her a little wary, but so far he'd not pushed it. The slamming doors of Jeremiah's truck brought her out of her thoughts.

"Cali," Jeremiah greeted, stepping out of his truck.

He was an affable bear, a big man with a barrel chest who wore an easy smile and had a gentle way about himself. Gray hair was threaded throughout his full beard. He came every morning with fruit and vegetables for the restaurant. It had taken her some time to get used to the way the local clan ran the town. There was a lot of bartering, and a lot of haggling over price for fun, much like one would imagine in older days passed. The clan worked together and provided for each other.

Jeremiah's son, Patrick, stepped out of the other side and she gave him a wave.

"What are you doing home?" She remembered making a cake for his going away party for college.

"I'm calling it a mental health break," Patrick laughed.

"College is tough," she agreed.

"That it is. I'm just here for a few days. I needed some skin time."

Cali nodded. She'd run into a few bears out, in their skin, as they called it. Selena had warned her, when Calita had first moved into town, that outside of the city proper, she would encounter bears as they regularly walked around in their skin. Shifters weren't allowed to do it in the populated city areas, but once past their small downtown, it was normal to see bears ambling along the sides of the two-lane road.

"Well, I'm sure your mother is ecstatic to have you home."

"Mama bears, what can I say?" He grinned.

She had to laugh at his charming smile. She shook her head and went to examine their inventory. She was complimenting him on the stuff that he brought. Approving it, she moved aside and allowed them to load it into the kitchen.

There was nothing like the produce in this town. She didn't know if it was the soil, or the natural way in which the bears tended to their plants, but she loved it. She'd come to town expecting the bears to be carnivores, but she'd been pleasantly surprised to find that while they ate meat, the people in this town loved the vegetarian meals she'd been able to add to the menu.

She'd been skeptical when Selena invited her to the town to work at her diner. After culinary school, she worked under her ex at his vegetarian restaurant. David had wanted to keep her close, and nothing was closer than his restaurant. He'd dismissed her pastries as housewife fare and made her focus on his dishes. She sighed and shook her head to dislodge those thoughts. Nearly a week of nightmares, she was done thinking about him. She was finally getting to bake for a living, and she wouldn't let thoughts of David derail her progress.

"We're all done, Calita," Patrick called behind her.

It pulled her attention and she turned to talk to him. His eyes widened and she frowned as he dived towards her. She screamed as he tackled her, not even hearing the crash as a satellite dish hit the ground in the exact spot she'd been standing. Her heart was in her throat as Patrick scrambled from on top her.

"Are…are you okay?" He held out his hand.

She stared a moment before she grabbed it. "What happened?"

"A satellite dish fell off the roof." He walked over and moved it out of the walkway.

The dish was small and rusted and looked like it hadn't been used in years. She turned and looked up at the roof of the diner. How in the world did it fall? But more importantly, how did it fall so close to her?

"How in the hell did you see it from inside the door?" She brushed off her pants.

"I didn't see it, I heard the air as it was coming down," Patrick explained, wiping his hands on his shirt.

His father came out the door with another employee hot on his tail. "We heard a scream, what happened?"

"I don't know, that thing fell off the roof," Patrick pointed at the rusted dish.

They all turned and looked at the roof. Fell seemed like the wrong word. She was a good two feet from the building, no way could it have reached her on its own. She shivered, and cursed her active imagination.

"That's so strange. I'll get someone to clean it up, are you okay, Chef?" One of the line cooks asked.

"Yeah," she murmured.

At least she thought so. Could she be overreacting? Either way, she didn't want to make a big deal of it. She waved off their concerned looks. Heart hammering, she walked back into the restaurant. She went back to making sure the fruit and vegetables were properly stored, her hands shaking the whole time. Every time she closed her eyes, she relived Patrick jumping towards her. For a moment she'd experienced, real, deep rooted fear and she'd been unable to move. It reminded her that she still had a long way to go. She would look into finding a therapist in the area. While she'd been doing a good job of holding herself together without the assistance, she knew having one would be good to help her with the changes in her life. Once she was done with the food delivery, she went upstairs. She needed to take a shower and get dressed before her meeting with Jerica. She was going to see her about the rental properties.

***

Hours later, she rushed into the kitchen and got to work on the evening pastries. She and Jerica had not only saw the small rentals available in the area, they'd also driven over to

Pleasant Hill to look at those apartments. The whole time Jerica hinted that Calita may not need a place to rent, but she ignored realtor. The whole town was full of meddlers and the real estate agent was no different.

She looked up as the kitchen door opened and butterflies attacked her stomach. Simon walked in, a pair of khaki chinos molded to his thighs and a jean button down shirt, loose, the top buttons opened. His hair was down around his shoulders, the curls windswept and tousled. It immediately made her think of the way he'd looked after their night together. She sucked in a sharp breath of need.

He smiled and came closer, his dark eyes raking her body. She leaned over as he got closer, offering her lips, as her hands were covered in flour and dough. He happily met her halfway, his tongue dipping into her mouth. Her body relaxed and energized at the same time.

She pulled back. "Hi. You got my message."

"I did. I was outside of cell range, sorry I missed your call," he whispered, sipping at her lips again.

She nodded her head towards a small table in the corner. "Sit, I'll be done in just a second."

He settled at the table and stretched his legs, his body language suggesting he was perfectly content to sit in her space. That made her incredibly happy. She finished the dish she was working on and ordered his favorite meal. It was a mushroom curry with spinach and chickpeas. She ordered parmesan corn fritters to go with it, and took a look at the honey pecan cheesecake she'd made for him that morning. It was her first time trying it, so she was anxious to see what he thought. She gave instructions to the staff and took off her apron.

She grabbed herself a glass of wine, knowing they were on the tail end of the dinner rush and that soon, she and the staff would start cleaning up. It was another thing she liked about small town living. There were no late nights. She would start the morning pastries when they were done and clean up after herself, leaving her and the bear, Anna, who'd deemed herself Calita's assistant, up a few hours after. She was usually done with everything a little after midnight depending on the next day's menu.

She sat at the table and Simon grabbed her hand. He brought it up to his mouth to kiss and frowned.

"Why do you smell like a male bear?" His voice was mild, but she saw his bear flash in his eyes.

"Jeesh, I've washed my hands at least a dozen times since then and changed my clothes," she muttered. "It's Patrick you smell, he saved my life today."

His frowned deepened. "I hadn't heard anything."

"It happened a few hours ago and only Patrick and his dad saw it. Even in this town, gossip doesn't travel if there is no one nosy to see it."

"What happened?"

"Something fell from the roof and Patrick grabbed me to keep it from hitting me. Freak accident." She worked to squelch her worry. She was calling it an accident and that was that.

His brows furrowed. "That's weird."

"I know. Patrick is a great kid, I'm glad he was there."

"I'll repay him for the favor. Your life is very important to me." He kissed her hand and released her.

***

An accident? Something about her manner didn't sit right with him. While her face was calm, her scent drifted to him, worry intermingled with her normal scent. It was a source of frustration for both he and his bear that they couldn't read her better. Calita was adept at hiding her feelings, something that made his bear leery and a little insecure. He studied her a moment more, but decided to drop it for now. He was just happy to be in her presence.

He'd settled his mind to spending the night in his skin, fighting to keep him and his bear from rushing her. So, when he had listened to her voicemail inviting him to come over, he'd rushed like the hounds of hell were after him. Calita was calling the shots, and Simon would stick to that, no matter what it cost him in cold showers. It had been a week since he last had his mate, and his bear was bucking at its leash.

He stared at her flushed face. She honestly took his breath away. Her hair was in its customary tight bun, but tendrils had escaped and were plastered to her neck, moist with sweat. His bear rumbled, as happy as Simon was to see her. When he'd come in, the sight of her at the counter had soothed him, yet made him tense with need. Her black jeans fit her thick thighs and cupped her ass in a way that had his cock twitching. It bucked against the zipper of his jeans even now.

The heat must've shown in his eyes, because her lips parted and she looked away. Her pulse quickened, her scent, beating even the delicious smells around the kitchen.

He changed the subject before he leaned over the table and devoured her. "Patrick's father was in the clan before my father passed. They're a good family."

She cleared her throat. "Most of the bears in this town are amazing. It must be great to have a pack so tight knit." She frowned and tilted her head. "Is it a pack of bears? What are a lot of bears called?"

He chuckled. "Technically, dictionary wise, it would be a sloth or sleuth of bears, but then we aren't normal bears, so we refer to ourselves as a clan."

She laughed "No, a sloth of bears?"

He pointed and gave her a mock glare. "Hold all jokes please."

She shrugged. "I mean, as slow as bears are, that's funny."

H laughed. "Don't mistake our easygoing manner. The saying that the only way you can escape a bear is by tripping your friend still applies."

She snickered. "How was your day?"

"Not much happening." He smiled at the young bear who brought up his dinner. He leaned down and inhaled. He loved the curry at Selena's. He held up a spoonful for her to try.

She waved away the offer with a smile.

"I know I spoke with you the night after your encounter with the cub, but I wanted to apologize again for how I treated you." He lifted his spoon and moaned at the first bite.

They talked every day since they slept together, and while he loved hearing her voice, he wanted to be with her.

"It's…" she shook her head and wound her fingers into the hand he was not using to eat. "It's settled. We discussed it."

"What made you step in to help?" He'd been curious about that.

Calita worried her bottom lip with her teeth, her brows pulling down as she thought about her answer. "It was almost a compulsion, if that makes sense." She wiped a hand over her face.

He hummed, because he knew what she meant, but of course she wouldn't yet understand the alpha female position.

"You been sleeping okay?" He changed the subject.

She smiled and avoided answering his question. "How did it go with the cub today?"

He sighed. He'd spent some time with the teenager, coaxing him through bonding with his emerging bear. "Cole's transitioning earlier than normal. He'll be a strong shifter. He has you to thank for him not losing it in the middle of downtown. If a bear changes in a chaotic episode like that, they could get trapped in their skin. Especially with him being so young. It's important to have family around during that first change."

She touched her chest. "I probably won't be doing that again."

"That would be a relief." He smiled and she returned his smile.

He dropped her hand and picked up his fork. "This is one of my favorites." He had a feeling she knew that.

"I heard a rumor it was."

He liked the smug look on her face. It was full of confidence and he was glad to see her opening up more.

She took a small sip of her wine. "What does being an alpha require?"

He shrugged and swallowed his food. "With these bears, not much. We have a great clan. We gather together most weekends and spend time together bonding. Our territory covers Clarke county, so it's mostly keeping out troublemakers and making sure my clan has what they need to be happy. Keeping the oversight committee away from our town is my main focus aside from that."

She nodded. "Sounds like a lot. What's the oversight committee do? I read about it online, but there's not much information about it."

He sighed, "When shifters first came out, if you remember, they separated us, put us on Sanctuaries and kept us from intermingling with humans."

"I read that you all had shifters in the government long before you came out." She sipped from her glass.

He nodded. "According to our history, we'd prepared to come out, but knew we'd need to have enough power amassed."

"They passed the apartheid laws anyway," she stated.

"Yes, and they lasted a decade before we could get them overturned. The negotiated truce included the oversight committee. Supposedly to keep both sides honest."

She snorted. "There's nothing honest about government."

He tipped his glass to her. "You are correct. Which is why I never want the greedy bastards near my county picking through our land like a toddler in a toy store." He'd seen more than his fair share of towns raided by the committee and he refused to let his clan fall victim to their greed.

"And how would you do that?"

"By keeping my bears out of trouble, and keeping humans from coming in here and starting it. I want nothing that would draw their attention, not territorial disputes, and definitely not 'human rights' issues. They use any excuse to confiscate land from an offending shifter party."

"I didn't know that," she murmured.

"You've had no reason to know that, darling."

She conceded his point and changed the subject. "I've been getting a few looks around town. Have you told people about us?"

He laughed. "Did you think it would take long for gossip to put us together?"

She shook her head, chagrined. It was a sport for the women in this town, her best friend included. It was inevitable for the rumors to spread. He would keep the tidbit about the bet to himself, knowing she'd feel some type of way about it.

"Besides, most of the gossip is about you helping Cole contain his bear."

She nodded, "yeah that too. Someone even addressed me as the alpha female. It's a little intimidating seeing as how I still don't know if I can be your mate."

"I'm a patient man."

She smiled dreamily. "I've noticed that about you."

"Is that why you haven't invited me over in a few days? The mating?"

"It has given me pause," she admitted. "But I've missed you."

He smiled and kissed the palm of her hand. She sighed in pleasure.

"I'm an alpha of a clan of bears. Trust me, waiting on my mate is nothing."

"What does that mean?"

He chuckled. "You've said it yourself. Bears are slow, in everything. You can't rush them, so believe me when I tell you dealing with a whole clan of them requires the upmost patience and tolerance."

"Well, I appreciate your patience."

He crooked his finger and she leaned in. He kissed her, unable to take another moment next to her without tasting her.

"Will you stay the night?" She whispered.

His bear banged against his subconscious and he purred, in total agreement with the animal. "For you, anything."

He finished off his dinner, enjoying the conversation with Calita. She let him do most of the talking which he was sure was strategic, but he let it happen. Until she was more comfortable with him, what more could he do? She brought out the most amazing cheesecake and watched him with happiness in her eyes as he devoured it.

She handed him the key to her room. "It will take me a couple of hours to be finished, but…wait for me?"

She had no idea how much she already had him wrapped around her fingers. Wait for her? He nearly laughed. She could ask anything of him and he'd probably say yes.

"Babe, without question." He gripped her chin and held her still for his questing tongue.

He backed away quickly, knowing he'd already stretched his bear's patience as far as it would tolerate. He left the kitchen, happy when he ran into Selena on the way out the door to his truck.

"Hey, Calita said she was almost hit with something falling off your roof. Do you know anything about that?"

Selena frowned, putting her hands on her hips. "Off the roof of the diner or the hotel?"

"The diner."

She shook her head. "I hadn't heard anything, but I'll look into it."

He thanked her and headed out to his truck. Anika had given him a box of candles that Calita had left after her ordeal with the young cub. He took them up to her room and set them up. He'd light them when she came home.

– 7 –

Calita stood outside of her hotel room door and breathed deep. The scent of the candles she'd chosen from Anika's shop drifted out to her and her shoulders relaxed. She was nervous, sure, but Simon had been true to his word. He hadn't pushed her. She opened the door and found him sitting in the small love seat adjacent to her bed, shirt and shoes off. The small flat screen on the wall was broadcasting a sports news show, the quiet voices of the anchors the only sound in the room. Candles were lit on the small bedside table, and dresser drawers in front of the bed.

She smiled at Simon's relaxed pose. He smiled and crooked his finger. He reached for her when she got close and pulled her into his lap. He nibbled along her chin and licked across her cheek.

"Hmm, sugar."

She snorted and stood. She needed to take a shower, she was sure sugar wasn't the only thing on her face and arms.

"Sit, Cali." He pointed at the small wooden table in front of him.

Her butt hit the surface of the table, obeying his order immediately. The smile he rewarded her with, sped her heartbeat. He lifted her leg and pulled off her tennis shoe. The sock was next, his fingers ghosting across her skin. He massaged her foot and she closed her eyes. Her body went pliant with every push into her heel. The scent of the candles, his touch, all of it lulled her into a place where she was floating. His chuckle brought her eyes open, he watched her, openly hungry for her. He kissed her heel and reached for her other foot, giving it the same ministration he'd given the other. Her body was putty by the time he'd finished.

He stood and held out his hand. "Come."

She was damn near close to it, but that wasn't what he meant, so she stood. He led her into the bathroom. And left her at the sink. He started the water and she could only stare. Did he think she was going to get into the shower with him? A streak of panic went through her and it brought his head up.

"What is it?" He moved to her and gripped her waist.

She shook her head. He sighed, but didn't push it. He pulled her T-shirt from her pants and started to lift it.

She stilled his hands. "I use the shower time to unwind, I..." How could she explain to him?

"My prudish mate," he murmured as he leaned over for a kiss.

She happily returned it.

"You need to come to my den so I can properly pamper you." He sipped at her lips.

Her heart beat picked up and she worried for a moment that he would start pushing for more than she was ready for. He kissed her softly and left the bathroom. She took a deep breath and ran a hand across her face. She'd invited him and she was messing up. Cali suppressed a growl and stripped, rushing into the shower stall in case he came back into the bathroom. Not that the frosted walls of the shower offered much privacy.

She quickly showered and cursed as she realized her clothes were in the other room. Grabbing the silk kimono on the back of the door, she slid her arms into it, cinching it tight. Her steps were slow, and tentative as she walked out of the bathroom. Simon was sitting on the edge of the bed, and for a moment she panicked. He'd put his shirt back on, and his shoes sat beside him as though he was getting ready to leave.

"Come here, Calita." His soft command carried across the room.

He made no moves, and no hint of what he was feeling showed on his face. She stopped in front of him. He parted his legs and pulled her between them. He ran his hands down her hips, the heat from his palms sinking through the silk. Her stomach did a slow roll as arousal flooded her body.

"I'm sorry, I didn't—"

"No, you don't apologize." He slid a hand up along her inner thigh. "You're calling the shots, Calita, but..."

She held her breath.

"You need to be sure you want me here. If you're not comfortable, I can leave."

"I don't want you to leave," she hastily said.

"Are you certain?" He trailed his fingers close to her sex and her mind fogged. "Calita?"

"I'm sure," she whispered.

He moved his hand from her skin and pulled her down into his lap. "Now, what about coming to my den scares you?"

It took a moment for his change of subject to register. She cleared her throat and closed the robe tighter. "I'm not scared, apprehensive maybe?"

He hummed and kissed her softly. "If you're going to give our relationship serious consideration, then we'll need to leave outside of these four walls."

He had a point, so she said nothing.

***

He sighed into her mouth, deepening their kiss. *Patience, patience,* he chanted in his head, whether it was for his bear who was quite peeved with their mate or himself, he didn't know. He said it to himself again for good measure to keep both reigned in. His mate needed it, he couldn't forget that.

She slid off his lap and crawled to the top of the bed. Seeing her bent over, was all it took to snap his control. He gripped her hips, pausing her before she could turn over and sit.

"Stay, just like that," he ordered.

She looked over her shoulder at him and every ounce of common sense fled his body. The picture she made…He damn near ripped his shirt as he snatched it off in his haste to get to her body. The khakis were next to be tossed behind him. His bear rumbled through his body as he ran his hands across Calita's thighs. He bunched the silk of her robe, pulling her hips back into his. She threw her head back and moaned as he positioned her at the head of his erection.

"Yes or no, love?" he whispered, desperate to be inside her.

She turned her head, and caught his eye. "Absolutely."

He pushed into her wet sheath, slow, drawing out every second. He closed his eyes and sighed in pleasure. Calita's head went back and the moan she released burrowed into his heart. He kept his strokes slow, savoring his mate. They still needed to continue their conversation, he wanted to push her for a more definitive answer. But with her every squeeze on his shaft that conversation got pushed back further and further. Once he had her, then his mind would clear and they could finish talking. Calita reached down and touched herself and that was all it took. His mind went blank, a haze of need descending. He pulled out, and her back arched, this time taking him deeper as he thrusted forward. Yeah, they could talk, much later.

***

He growled, low and long as his phone rang for a third time. Who in the hell was calling him this early on a Sunday? It was the only day he allowed himself to sleep in. He peeked open an eye and saw that it was a little after eight am. He sighed and rolled over, grabbing his phone off the bedside table.

"Yeah."

"Hey, Alpha, did I wake you? You're usually up—"

"What do you want?" Lord above, female bears were so extra.

"Well, I was looking for Calita's number."

He grunted. *Yeah right.* "Did you ask Selena?" He opened his eyes as Charmain got quiet.

"Full disclosure, I was driving by, and I saw your truck at the hotel so—"

"Oh for God's sake," he muttered.

Charmain snickered. "A few of the women were going to do brunch today in Pleasant Hill and we wanted to see if Calita wanted to join us."

He rolled his eyes and held his phone over his shoulder. He'd felt Calita wake moments ago. She sat up and gave him a startled look.

She grabbed his phone, but watched him. "What's going on?"

"Meddling." He kicked from under the blankets and headed for the shower.

There would be no morning sex for him. That much was clear. He sighed, extremely put upon, and his bear grumbled in agreement.

***

What in the world? She ignored the phone for a moment, watching Simon's ass, as he walked, unashamed, into her bathroom nude. How a man his size moved so fluidly put her in awe. She looked at the phone and brought it up to her ear. She stretched, her body deliciously loose and relaxed.

"Yes?"

"Hi, Calita, it's Charmain. I own the gas station not too far from the hotel." The woman's chipper voice put her at ease.

She racked her mind to put a face to the name. "Okay?"

"Well, a bunch of the ladies are having brunch over at Morton's in Pleasant Hill. They have bottomless mimosas and the most amazing waffles," Charmain sighed gustily.

Any hesitance she would've felt disappeared under the excitement in the other woman's voice. She hadn't had friends in a while, and besides Selena and Anika, she hardly knew any of other women in the clan. She could probably count the amount of friends she had ever had on one hand. In high school, she and Selena had stuck to themselves, and the one year she'd finished of college, she'd spent it wishing she was home, so she had not made any new friends.

There were some fellow chefs from the culinary school she went to, but David had been so controlling, and her work schedule so hectic they soon fell to the way side. She'd been in town for a year, it was time she started making new friends.

"Calita?" Charmain prodded.

"Yes, I'd love to. What time?"

"Well, there are a total of ten of us, so we're carpooling. Do you want one of us to come get you?"

"No, that's okay. I can drive myself." It would give her an excuse to leave in case she and the women didn't get along.

"Okay, great! We're meeting there at ten."

She glanced at the clock and calculated how long it would take her to get dressed. "That's perfect. I'll see you then."

"I'm so excited, see you then."

She smiled and ended the call. Simon came out of the bathroom dressed, his hair wet from a quick shower.

He leaned over the bed and kissed her lips. "What are you doing today?"

She handed him his phone. "I'm going to brunch with a few of your bears."

He snorted. "They're meddling."

"Of course," she agreed, and found herself unable to be upset with that.

In the year she'd been in town, she didn't have much personal experience with their meddling. She was an outsider, a great chef who cooked well, but an outsider all the same. It didn't help that she'd held back from Bear Ridge's residents, not sure she'd stay in town as long as she had. She was happy to be invited even if it was just because she was dating their alpha.

She dragged the sheet up to cover her body and scrambled from the bed. "I gotta get dressed." She shooed him with a kiss and a push on his shoulder.

"Don't let them interrogate you."

"My secrets are my own," she said over her shoulder.

"True enough," he grumbled.

Guilt niggled. There were a lot of things he didn't know about her. If she decided to give it a go at being his mate, then she would need to tell him at some point. She shook out that morose thought. She was going to brunch, and possibly making more friends. It was time to get out of her shell and live. She couldn't let her past control her life anymore.

$$- 8 -$$

An hour later, Cali left her room anticipating brunch. She was excited and she realized, happy. With Simon lying next to her, she'd slept dream free in what felt like forever. Optimism, something she'd not felt in years buoyed her. She was walking through the lobby when the clerk waved her down. She was on the phone, so Cali waited patiently at the counter until she finished. Tessa was typing away as she approached.

"Yes, I have it. A week, what's the name for the reservation. David Barnes, can you spell that?"

Calita's body went cold, her hands started trembling. There were plenty of men named David in the country. It could be purely coincidental. Nevertheless, she found herself debating whether or not to cancel brunch with her potential friends. Anxiety churned her stomach, and her skin prickled. She took a deep breath as the clerk hung up and smiled at her.

"Hey, I have a message for you. You're supposed to meet Charmain and the ladies in Hilton at…" Tessa picked up a little sticky note, "the Grand Ellis, for brunch and not Morton's."

Calita nodded, her face frozen with a fake smile as though she wasn't nearing a panic attack. "All the way over in Hilton?"

Tessa smiled. "I know right, fancy."

She'd have to plug it into her GPS. They were going to meet her there, she couldn't in good conscious cancel. She sighed "Thank you."

She walked out to her barely used vehicle and climbed in. She didn't bother downing the window to let the heat out since chills raced through her body. She put her head on the steering wheel for a moment to catch her breath. No way would David use his real name to check into the hotel. It would be stupid. He was on the run from the law. Her brain processed the logic, but her body was in full freak out mode. She swallowed and looked back up towards her room. She should just go back upstairs, forget brunch. She could dig through her paperwork and call the detectives that had worked her case and let them know he was here. She grabbed the door handle, intending to do that but the more she thought on it, the crazier it seemed. She hadn't even heard the whole conversation. Didn't even know when this David would check in.

Would she spend her free time holed in her room on the off chance that it was him?

She came to Georgia for a new life, she would not let old fears rule her. Taking a shaky breath, she pulled out of the hotel parking lot and turned onto the main road leading out of town. She managed to calm herself by the time she'd gone a few miles. There was nothing but trees on either side of the two-lane road, she'd learned early on that cell coverage was a joke on this stretch. It was one of the reasons she actively avoided driving to Hilton alone. Driving the deserted stretch made her nervous. She much preferred the other route out of town. That way at least had small clusters of houses in between the towns.

Glancing up into her rearview mirror, she frowned as a blue car came barreling down on hers. Why in the hell were they driving so fast? There was a blind turn coming up, and no way was she taking it faster than the fifty-five miles an hour she was driving. They would have to pass her.

She'd grown up in Chicago, taking the train and bus everywhere she needed to go. She barely drove as an adult and according to Selena she drove like an old lady. The car rushed up to her bumper and started blowing the horn. She frowned and looked into the car to see who it was. All she saw was a figure in big shades, a hat and…. a sweatshirt, in this heat? She couldn't tell if it was a man or a woman. Calita slowed down. There were double lines, but hopefully they would just go around her. The turn was coming up so she slowed down to forty. The car tapped her bumper and let out a blast on the horn. She squealed as the car bumped her again, this time harder. Speeding to avoid another bump, she swallowed a scream as the car tires screeched into the turn.

The blue car hit her on the corner of her bumper sending her careening into the other lane. Calita turned sharply on the wheel to get back into the correct lane and sent the car into a fishtail. Trees were coming up quickly, she slammed on the breaks and pulled the wheel. Her car swerved into the dirt embankment avoiding the tree head on, but she careened into it with the driver's side backseat. Her car sputtered and died, and silence blanketed the morning.

Stunned from the impact of the airbag, shock kept her in place, her breathing erratic. Smoke was seeping from the hood of her car and it spurred her into action. She didn't know if it would catch on fire. She tried to open the driver's side door, but the tree had bent the frame of her car, sealing the door in place. Grabbing her purse from the middle console, she climbed over to the passenger side. Gingerly, she worked her way out of the car. She wiped a shaking hand down her face, gasping at the blood covering her fingers. A sob escaped and searing heat went through her chest with every breath she took. Her legs gave out, and she sat on the ground hard. She could've died, and as she looked around, she realized the person who'd caused the accident was nowhere to be found.

With shaking hands, she pulled her phone out of her purse, whimpering as she bent her wrist. History told her it was sprained and not broken, but it still hurt. She'd had more than one sprained wrist in her relationship with David, so she blocked out that pain to lift her phone. There were no bars. God, there was another mile before she would get a signal. She needed to get up and move, or she'd be stranded on the side of the road. Though it was morning, the heat would no doubt climb, threatening her with heat exhaustion. She went to stand and cried out in pain, as she put weight on her sprained wrist. She fell back into the soft dirt of the shoulder.

It took her two more tries to stand. She froze at the rustling sound nearing her car. Heart in her throat, she waited. A bear shuffled from the woods and circled her car. Real bear or shifter, she couldn't remember how to tell, and she didn't want to risk calling out. Backing up, she cursed as she stepped on the dry leaves scattered across the ground. The crunching sound alerted the bear and his head whipped to her. He lifted his snout and sniffed. Standing on two legs he transformed in front of her. She quickly averted her eyes from him once mahogany skin replaced the fur. She recognized the veterinarian that came into the diner often.

"Are you okay?" Marcus asked, his voice gruff.

She swallowed and nodded. She turned her head as he continued to stand there with his legs apart, hands on his hips. She put up a hand to cover his privates from her gaze.

"Yes, I'm okay. Just some minor injuries."

He stared at her a moment. "Of course, I only work on animals, but that gash on your forehead probably needs some stitches." He turned to examine her car. "What happened?"

"Someone ran me off the road."

He spun back around. "Did you see who it was?"

She shook her head.

He growled. "My clothes and phone are back a few miles, I can make the distance in my skin faster, but the alpha would kill me if I left you here alone. Do you have a phone on you?"

She nodded.

"Well, we should be able to get a signal a little ways up the road, are you okay to walk?"

"Yeah, I can walk." She winced.

He started towards her, and she backed away. "You're just going to walk naked?"

He looked confused for a moment, then shook his head. "I forget how prudish humans are. If it will make you feel better, I can get in my skin."

She didn't relish walking next to a bear for the next mile. She wanted the human contact more than anything. "I have an apron in the backseat of my car," she offered.

He laughed. "Your call." He opened the back door and grabbed the apron and tied it around his waist. "Better?"

She lowered her hands. His built chest was still bare, the apron only covering his waist. "It's silly, I know, but thank you."

He smiled, an easy flash of teeth that put her further at ease. "Come, let's get you some help."

They set off down the highway, her gait slow and stiff. He growled a moment before swinging her up into his arms. She screamed in pain and he loosened his grip. She lay stiff in his arms for the first ten steps, but he ignored her panicked breaths and oddly it calmed her. She slowly relaxed and he grunted in acknowledgment, but said nothing else.

***

Simon rubbed the back of his neck as his bear slammed into his subconscious. He was supposed to be going over requests to join his clan from other bears, but he was having a hard time concentrating on work this morning. His bear was restless, growling and prowling through his body.

Mate.

That thought circled Simon's head as his bear made its needs known. *I want her too, trust me, I do, but we have to be patient with her. We left her just this morning, and we'll go see her again as soon as she gets off tonight.*

Mate.

Simon growled, frustrated with his bear's stubbornness. He would need to get in his skin soon if he wasn't able to control the damn beast.

His beta looked up. "Alpha?"

"Sorry, a disagreement with my bear."

Gavin smiled. They both looked up as one of his enforcers knocked on his office door.

"Alpha, we had some trespassing. From the scent, it happened last night."

He leaned back in his chair and frowned. "Trespassing?" Could that be the source of his uneasiness?

"Along the east boundary." His enforcer reported.

"Shifter?"

"Both a shifter and a hybrid female by the scent."

He growled. She wouldn't dare. What would be Miranda's reason for skulking around his property? But who else? Was she with the male he saw her with?

"Is the scent still there?" Gavin asked.

"Faint, but yes."

He and Gavin shared a look. "I'll check it out, you keep going through those applications."

Gavin sucked his teeth and Simon smiled. Neither of them wanted to go through the paperwork involved with potential new clan members. It was a tedious task, but necessary to keep troublemakers out of their clan. He went outside the barn where he housed his offices and jumped on the back of the ATV parked there. His enforcer jumped on the other and they headed towards the eastern boundary of their property. They got off their four wheelers and he sniffed the air. It was faint as his enforcer said, but it was Miranda's scent, along with the scent of the other male. What could she possibly be thinking? He followed the scent on foot and off of his land about a half a mile before he turned around. He was satisfied that their scent seemed to be headed off clan land, and not further in. He turned back.

"Keep an eye out for her. I don't like it," he told his enforcer as he jumped back on his ATV. He gave him a description and promised to text out her picture to the rest of the enforcers guarding their borders who didn't remember how she looked.

He took his time getting back to the office, his anxiety ramping up the closer he got to his barn. What was going on with his bear? Gavin rushed up to him as he got closer. A worried expression covered his beta's face.

"I was just about to come and get you."

"What's happened?" He turned off the ATV and hopped off. "What is it?"

He asked the question, but his bear swiped at him, he knew it was about their mate. His breath stalled. "Calita?"

Gavin nodded. "In a car accident. She's at the clinic."

No!

He turned inward about to let his bear out, but his beta grabbed his arm.

"We'll get there faster in the truck."

He nodded, it made sense. He could travel fast in his skin, but the truck would travel faster. He jumped in the passenger seat since Gavin had already jumped in the driver seat and started the engine.

They made it to the small town clinic in no time and he rushed through the doors. The receptionist pointed, though he didn't need it. He'd picked up his mate's scent from the moment he opened the doors. He found her in one of the exam rooms getting stitches. He hissed, his eyes cataloguing the bandage wrapped around her wrist and the one peeking from under her t-shirt. Her eyes were closed, her lips pinched in pain. Her distress brought a growl to his throat.

Her eyes popped open and widened. "Simon," she whispered his name and he was at her side.

He watched the slow bear put in a final stitch, taking his sweet time. He wanted to growl at the male to go faster, but knew it would make no difference. Once the doctor tied it off, Simon moved him aside and leaned down to hug Calita. She hissed in pain.

"I'm sorry, my love." He pulled back from the exam table. "What happened?"

"Someone ran me off the road."

He snarled, the sound menacing and filling the small room. Calita's heart rate increased. He sucked in a deep breath to calm down. *Our mate is here and safe,* he reassured his bear. The doctor ignored his growling, handing Simon a bandage and pointing at Calita's wound. It strangely calmed Simon as he did as the doctor ordered. Instead of questioning Cali further, he would visit Nate after he got her settled.

"Is she free to go?"

The doc nodded. "I gave her something for the pain, though she'll feel it more tomorrow. I called in a prescription for you, I suggest you take it before you go to bed tonight, Calita."

She nodded and winced.

"Give your wrist a day before you start using it. Nothing is broken, so the tenderness along your ribs are likely bruises and will go away in a couple of weeks. Try not to lift anything for about a week to give your body a break. Two would be better, but, if you're anything like Selena, that's asking for a lot to stay out the kitchen that long."

"She'll rest," Simon assured him and earned a glare from his mate.

Calita cut her eyes at him and sighed.

"Selena can make do without you for a few days." He softened his voice.

"I'm not sitting around doing nothing for a week." She grumbled.

He crowded her space and her scent changed, immediately a spike of fear intertwined with her wariness. She squashed it so fast, he was confused as to whether or not he'd really smelled it. He backed up anyway, holding up his hands, suppressing a frustrated growl.

"I just think it best if you follow the doctor's orders."

"I don't want to argue with you, Simon. I'll be fine in a few days. For now, I just…I need to get out of here." Her breath was speeding up, her eyes darting around the room in nervousness.

She moved to sit up on the examining table, nimbly, as though used to moving about with injuries. He had a pretty good idea why and it did nothing to cool his worry. He tamped down on his anger. He couldn't let his mind dwell on what could've happened to her in the past, not when she needed him now. Calita climbed down off the table and he rushed to her side to help. He was relieved when she didn't pull away from him.

He walked her to his truck and his beta handed him the keys. He paused before cranking up the car.

"I would really like to take you to my house and take care of you."

She looked up at him, her eyes hazy from the pain meds, but nonetheless wary. "I'd feel a little more relaxed in my own space."

He nodded, and started the engine. "I'll get you settled, then go out for your pain meds. Can I get you anything else while I'm out?"

She looked at him, her lips parted in shock. "You aren't going to argue?"

"About what, sweetheart?"

"About the fact that I don't want to go home with you."

He turned to face her. "Calita, I don't know what your past relationships were like, but I'm not them. Am I bossy, yes, controlling, absolutely not. You want to rest at home, I'll take you home."

Wonder filled her face. "Thank you. I would appreciate it."

He grabbed her chin. "You're my mate, so naturally I want you in my den where I can make sure nothing happens to you, but your comfort is always a top priority for me."

She grabbed his arm and nuzzled into his hand.

"One day, you'll tell me about the shadows lingering in your eyes, yes?"

She sighed, kissed his palm and nodded. She turned from him and stared out the window.

He wanted her secrets, but he wanted her willing to give them to him. Like he told Nate, he wanted his mate's trust. He drove her straight to the hotel and with much protesting from her, carried her up to her room. Once he had her settled, he went to the drugstore to fill her prescription. There was already talk about the accident, his bears stopping him to ask how she was doing. He took a trip to buy her candles and flowers and headed back to her hotel. He was staying the night to keep an eye on his mate. Hopefully she wouldn't argue with him about it.

– 9 –

Simon woke before Calita the next morning, and quietly left the bed. He left a quick note on the dresser so as not to worry her and got dressed. He walked the short distance to the sheriff's office and marched passed the deputies quietly working at their desks, straight back to Nate's office. He gave a cursory knock before walking into the small space. There was room enough for the large teak desk his cousin sat behind, as well as a metal filing cabinet that had seen better days. Another relic from their uncle, no doubt, along with the carved wooden figures that adorned the top of it. The curtains were open, flooding sunlight into the room.

"Alpha," Nate said, sipping his coffee.

He frowned and sniffed, smelling the overly sweet latte. "Why are you drinking that crap?"

Nate set down his cup. "You're asking why, I, a bear with a sweet tooth, would drink this?"

Simon shrugged, conceding his cousin's point. He sat down in the leather bucket chair in front of the sheriff's desk. "Any word on Calita's car accident?"

Nate sat back in his chair and intertwined his fingers on his chest. "There are marks on the back of her car that confirms she'd been hit. Whether accident or on purpose remains to be seen. There are skid marks from her car, but only one set, so clearly whoever hit her didn't stop."

Simon growled. "How bad was it?"

Nate was quiet for a moment, as he considered his answer. "She's lucky," he said finally.

Simon stood and paced the small office. "What are you doing about it?"

"We're canvassing the town for blue cars with front end damage. If we don't find anything here, we'll check the next town. I've also put out a bolo to the other sheriff stations. Hopefully we'll hear something back."

He nodded, relaxing marginally. Nate was good at his job, so yelling at his cousin wouldn't help anything. With the way gossip moved through their town, no way would someone miss a dented car. They were already buzzing at the drugstore when he went yesterday. He sat down and went over his thoughts for a moment.

"The other day, she was almost hit with a satellite dish falling from Selena's roof."

Nate nodded. "Selena told me."

"Do you think the two could be related?"

He hummed and sat up, clasping his hands together, elbows on his desk. "I'll go look around myself."

"While you're looking into that, Miranda brought a bear into our territory without proper paperwork."

"Really?" Nate froze. "Name?"

"Charles Rossel."

He'd assigned a couple of his enforcers to keep a general eye out for both Miranda and Charles, but so far, they hadn't done anything to warrant him kicking them out of town. He thought about the trespassing from the night before.

"I'll run him and put some feelers out." Nate said calmly.

"They've been lurking around the property and you know how I am about that."

"No doubt. I'll let you know if I find anything."

Satisfied that Nate would look into it, he headed back to the hotel. He stopped in the restaurant and grabbed breakfast for Calita, answering more questions about her health. She was still sleep by the time he slipped into her room. He set the breakfast tray on the bedside table. He walked through the sitting area and pulled back the curtains to let in a little light. She rolled over and groaned. Walking back to the bed, he picked up and shook her pill bottle.

"Body sore?" he asked.

Another groan was his answer. He tapped out two pain pills and held out his hand. She grabbed them gratefully, grabbing the orange juice from the tray. He waited a beat until she'd swallowed them down.

"I brought you breakfast."

"Thank you." Her voice was hoarse and gravelly.

He kissed her temple. He didn't want to leave, but he'd volunteered himself to give a trail ride to allow one of his bears a day off. "I need to get to work, will you be okay today?"

She hummed, in answer.

"Is that a yes or no, sweetheart?"

She frowned, her eyes still at half-mast of sleep. "I'll be fine."

He nodded and gave her a small kiss. "Call me if you need anything, no matter what."

She hummed again and settled back into the blankets before rolling over.

***

Calita cracked open an eye and winced at the sun coming in through the curtains. She always left them closed, why were they opened? She was groggy and sore as hell as she worked to sit up in the bed. Her head was throbbing as she turned and spotted the tray Simon had left for her on the table. That's right. She remembered waking when he'd come back in. Giving the tray a critical glance, she debated eating. The heavy painkillers she was taking demanded she put something on her stomach. She groaned and reached for the tray.

She'd finished the last bite of fruit when someone knocked on the door of her room. She sighed and gingerly shuffled from the bed. Two women stood at the door, a large bouquet in their hands, their faces expectant.

"Yes?"

The women shared a look. One stepped forward. "I'm Charmain, we were supposed to have brunch together yesterday. This is Meghan."

"Of course, come in please." She stepped back and allowed them entrance.

They dragged in a hand full of floating balloons behind them. "You poor thing," Charmain tsked.

"We were at the drugstore yesterday and heard about your accident. Lie down, we'll take care of this for you." Meghan guided her back to the edge of her bed.

She was still dazed with sleep and docile as she went along with Meghan.

"Thank you." Cali grabbed the balloons as the woman passed her. "You guys didn't have to do this."

"Nonsense." Charmain set up the flowers on the coffee table. "We were worried when you didn't make it to Morton's. Imagine our surprise when we heard Marcus found you headed in the opposite direction."

"Where were you going?" Meghan asked. Curiosity had them both on the edge of the chairs in which they sat.

She looked between them confused. "You guys are messing with me, right?"

Charmain frowned. "What do you mean?"

"I got a message from the front desk that said you'd changed the restaurant."

"What?" Meghan shared a look with Charmain. "No, everyone knows Morton's has the best brunch. They are the fanciest place within fifty miles of this place."

Silence fell between them as they all shared a confused look.

"I wonder who called," Meghan murmured after a moment of awkward silence.

She walked over to the landline in the room, next to the bed and called down to the front desk. Meghan spoke with Tessa a few moments and hung up frowning. "That's very odd, she said one of us called."

"Did she give a name?" Charmain sat forward in her chair.

Meghan shook her head. "Do you think it was done on purpose?"

Charmain looked to Calita. "I don't see why, who would want to hurt you?"

Cali's blood went cold and she started trembling. She put her hand to her head.

"You know what guys, I'm not feeling very well. I think I will lay down and take a nap," she whispered.

Meghan clucked in sympathy. "Of course, of course. Let us get out of your hair."

She and Charmain left and Cali stayed put on the edge of the bed, her mind spinning. Hard trembles wracked her body as she went over the events from yesterday. A knock on the door preceded Selena as she walked into the room without waiting. She rushed to Cali's side.

"What's happened?" Selena brushed a hand across her forehead.

Cali shuddered. "Someone called yesterday and told me that they changed the restaurant."

Selena frowned. "What are you talking about?"

"Someone ran me off the road on purpose."

Shit. Shit. Calita chest tightened as panic threatened to overtake her.

Selena reared back. "That's...he doesn't know you're here." Her best friend spoke aloud what Cali was too afraid to articulate.

She didn't want to think about David being here. She told Selena about the call she overheard at the front desk.

"Have you told Simon?"

She clutched Selena's arm. "I haven't." She swallowed. "I have to tell him now, don't I?"

Selena stood and paced away. "I don't keep things from my mate, Cali. Once I tell Nathan…" She sighed. "Simon is the alpha, and Nate will probably tell him you think you're in danger. I know Nate looked into it when you got here." She held up her hand as Calita tried to protest. "He's in charge of keeping trouble out of this town, Cali."

"What did he say he found?"

"He wouldn't tell me anything, Nate's serious about privacy."

Calita let out a relieved breath. She couldn't help the sting of tears. She didn't want to relive it, but if Simon really thought she was his mate, it was best to tell him before he invested too much into her. She could never be what he needed.

Selena frowned. "I know it feels impossible, Cali, but trust Simon, it will be alright."

Cali nodded.

"In the meantime, why don't you come stay with Nate and me? Just on the off chance that it really is David. I don't believe he would be so stupid, but you'll never rest with the possibility hanging over your head."

"Selena," she sighed. "I can't impose." Simon had invited her out to his home, maybe she would take him up on the offer.

"You can't stay here, Cali." Her best friend insisted.

"I can go to Simon's."

Selena nodded, "that's a great idea, I'll help you pack. We can go to the sheriff's office and then call him when you're done."

Selena was in full bullying mode; Cali knew telling her no would be useless. She let out a huff of breath and got up from the bed. She shuffled to her closet and threw some clothes into an overnight bag. Selena helped her down the stairs and out the door. Though the sheriff's office was only a few doors down from the motel, they drove. Nate was sitting behind his desk, scowling at the computer. He stood when they entered.

He grabbed her other arm and helped her into the chair in front of his desk. "You want a more comfortable chair?"

Nate's voice was quiet, firm. He had an easy way about him. He'd put her at ease within the first few minutes of meeting him when she'd first moved to town. She shook her head. He walked over to his mate and nuzzled her before going back to his seat.

His serious gaze studied Calita as he settled into his chair. "How are you feeling?"

She shrugged, "I imagine I look exactly how I feel."

His lips quirked up.

"You hear anything else about my accident?"

"Nothing has happened since I talked to you yesterday."

She cleared her throat and shored up her courage. "That's not the only reason I came. I wanted to know about David. To see if you could look into finding him."

He stared a moment before he turned around and pulled a file from the cabinet. He opened it on his desk and typed a couple of things into his computer. "He's still in prison."

Her heart thudded and her ears rang. "How long?" She finally managed to whisper.

"They caught him three years ago for assaulting another woman, one of a string of women."

Her heart thudded. Three years. She was still in Chicago struggling to get out of bed three years ago and he'd been in prison. "This whole time?"

"I assumed you knew since it happened while you were still in Chicago." He closed the file on his desk.

"You looked into it?"

"I do background checks on all new residents." He shrugged.

He didn't look remorseful, and she couldn't really blame him. Though there was finally peace between shifters and humans, there was still tensions between the two groups.

"So, it definitely wasn't him yesterday." She ran a shaking hand through her hair.

He lowered his brows. "What would make you think that?"

She told him what she'd told Selena.

He leaned forward on his desk. "You didn't tell me this yesterday. I did wonder why you were going in the other direction. Morton's is the brunch spot in these parts. What time was the call?"

"A little after nine, yesterday morning."

"And you were supposed to meet Charmain and Meghan?"

She nodded.

He hummed. "Anything else?"

She shook her head.

"Okay, let me know if you think of anything else, or something else happens that makes you uncomfortable."

"I will." She stood and he stood up to come around the desk. She waved him away. "I got it."

She left the station with Selena, pulling out her phone to call Simon. Though he'd talked about her coming out to his ranch, she didn't want to assume. She'd ask him about staying and then get Selena to drop her off. Her stomach fluttered, settling as she spotted Simon standing outside of the station. He was propped against his truck, arms over his chest and legs crossed.

"Oh yeah, I already called Simon," Selena informed her. Her best friend walked ahead of her and went to her car. She took Calita's suitcase out of her trunk and opened Simon's cab door, depositing her things. Selena waved as she bypassed the car they'd drove over and headed to the diner.

Simon watched Calita, his head tilted as his gaze assessed her. He opened his arms after a moment and she shuffled into them. She sighed, she needed pain pills, but seeing him outside was a balm to her soul. She needed to tell him about David and all the other things that were making her uncomfortable, but for now, she enjoyed the heat of his body.

Simon lifted her chin. "Home or with me?"

"With you," she whispered.

He made a chuffing sound and kissed her hair. She hid her smile as he lifted her, cradling her into his body.

– *10* –

Simon smiled and kissed the top of Calita's head again. She finally agreed to come home with him. His bear purred. When Selena called, he'd been worried, so he'd rushed over. Calita coming out of the sheriff's department hadn't helped, but as soon as he saw her, his bear had calmed. He settled her into the passenger seat of his truck. There was the acrid taste of fear surrounding her and he was confused.

He brushed a hand over her cheek. "What's wrong?"

"Why do you ask?" She kissed his palm.

"I can sense your moods and right now you're all over the place, but fear is there and that worries me."

She shook her head. "I packed for the whole week, is that okay?"

Deflecting the subject as usual. He squelched his irritation. "Calita."

She shook her head. "Let's go. I need… I need to get out of here."

He nodded, and backed away. The hair on the back of his neck stood up and he knew they were being watched. He shut her door gently and took a look around. Charles was lounging against the railing in the front of Selena's restaurant. Simon narrowed his eyes as the guy gave him a salute. Miranda gave him a nasty look and turned her back. He would check with his contacts to see if they'd heard anything about the bear.

Something didn't sit right with him about the male. In the meantime, he sent a text message to Nate.

He got in the car and pulled out of the station parking lot, putting them from his mind. Instead, he focused on his mate. She was solemn, her head against the glass as they traveled down the two lane road that led out of Bear Ridge. Once they passed the vet's office, the houses were sparser, until there was nothing but green on either side of the road. They ascended and descended the hilly countryside that led to his ranch. Calita became increasingly tense, the further they got from town. He pulled the car over, putting it in park on the shoulder tourists used as a lookout.

He turned to her. "Spill it."

Her eyes widened. The tension in the car racked up another notch and Simon had to wrangle his bear under control.

"Something is bothering you and I want to know what it is before you get to my den." She sighed and he hurried to assure her. "If you're apprehensive, this can wait until you're ready. Bears are easy going, but it takes nothing to startle them. You walking onto my land as nervous and skittish as you are will put them instantly on edge. Especially since I am on edge."

She cleared her throat. "I…" she stopped, and he read the confusion on her face.

"I can handle whatever it is, my love."

She stared into his eyes, tears gathering in hers.

"So I should turn around?"

She shook her head, sighed and unbuttoned the flannel she wore. He watched her, his frown deepening as she unbuttoned past her bra and opened the shirt. She winced as she pulled up her tank top. It was then he noticed the scars running along the top her stomach, disappearing under her breasts. These were not new scars, so they most definitely didn't come from her car accident. His hands shook as he moved her shirt off her shoulder to get a better look. The scars went underneath her bra and he wondered exactly how much he'd missed in his haste to have her. He realized he hadn't seen her fully naked. He felt callous, a brute.

"How did I miss these? I feel like an ass."

She placed her hand atop his. "I hid them on purpose. I never took off my shirt, just moved it down, I didn't want you to see them."

"What happened?" His trembling fingers traced the light patchwork across her skin.

She flinched. He raised his eyes to hers trying to read the fear and anxiety that filled the car.

"I finally decided to leave my abusive boyfriend…he took exception to that."

The stark recitation of the words sent his bear into a tailspin. He breathed deep through his nostrils. Still, the animal thrashed against his control, his head pounding as it fought to come out. To say bears were protective of women and children was an understatement, and his bear was having a hard time with its mate having been abused.

"Is he dead?" His growl filled the truck's interior with its menacing sound.

Her lids lowered, and she let out a shuddering breath and shook her head.

"Where is he?"

"My neighbor intervened. He ran."

He unbuckled her seat belt and moved his seat back before pulling her across the center console and into his arms.

"By the time I left the hospital, the police were unable to find him. After a few months my case was shuffled to the bottom. I don't know if they ever really looked for him. It's why I eventually left Chicago. I didn't feel safe with him on the loose." She shuddered in his arms.

He kissed her hair, "I want to know who he is, and then you put it out of your mind. He will never lay another hand on you."

She put a hand up against his chest. "I just talked to Nate, and it turns out he's been in jail. I…I've been scared for my life for three years, and he's been locked up in another city." She shuddered. "For long moments this morning, I thought he was here."

"Because of what happened to you?"

She shook her head. "Not just that. I overheard a call from the receptionist. It was a David, clearly in light of this, a coincidence, but then someone ran me off the road." Her breath quickened, the acrid scent of panic flooding the truck. "Oh God, I thought he was back," she whispered.

He lost control, hissing as his bear clawed at his insides demanding to be let out. The hair exploded on his arms, claws piercing his skin as his bear nearly forced his change. She scrambled out of his lap and pushed herself back into the passenger door. Her fear calmed down his bear, the animal understanding he was the cause.

"Don't cower from me, Calita, please. I would never hurt you." His voice was a deep timbre.

"I'm not afraid of you…per se. I don't want to be in your lap if you turn into a bear."

He nodded, understanding how sensitive she had to be with everything that had happened. He closed his eyes and breathed deep. It took him a few minutes to calm both he and his bear. He gripped the steering wheel of his truck and leaned his head against it. Shuddering, he suppressed another growl and reigned in control. It had been years since his bear had been so wildly unmanageable. She mewled, and he closed his eyes. Of course, she would be able to feel his rage, despite his efforts to reign it in. He felt like an ass, she was scared and he was making her fear about him. He breathed out and sat straight. He unbuckled his seat belt and held his arms out to her. She came into his arms easily, assuaging some of his anxiety.

"I'm sorry you went through that today, Calita."

He held her for a few minutes, rubbing his cheek along the top of her hair, calming them both. He kissed the top of her head after a while and she moved back into her seat. Once she was buckled in, he checked his mirrors and pulled out onto the empty road.

The silence was tense as they rode the rest of the way to his land. He pulled into his garage and sighed. She unbuckled her seat belt and went to reach for her bag in the back seat, but he lifted her over the console and into his lap. Her surprised gasp brushed his neck and his whole body tightened.

He held her in his lap, fighting the images in his mind of her being attacked. She squirmed after a minute.

"Wait, Cali. I just need a minute."

"It was over four years ago, Simon. I've been getting better since I moved here."

He put his hand over her mouth. "That doesn't help me."

She raised her eyebrows. He was waging a battle with himself and what she thought was reassuring was anything but. That after four years, she was still battling with the trauma was shredding his insides. He fought the need to demand she move in with him. On his land, his entire clan would be able to keep an eye on her, but somehow, he didn't think she was ready for that.

He breathed in her scent and after a few minutes calmed himself. He put his head against her forehead.

"Is that why you talked to Nate?"

She backed up. "He already knew about David being in jail…when I came down, I told Selena. You know how she is."

He nodded. Selena was loyal to a fault, and though meddlesome, her intentions were always good. He knew the woman wouldn't have left her friend to go through the trauma alone. Nate knowing, explained his cousin's reluctance to give him information on Calita. He didn't want to break his mate's confidence; Simon could understand that.

"So, you told Nate you thought David was back?"

She looked away.

"Calita."

"There has been a couple accidents. I attributed them to David, but he's in jail now, so…" She shrugged.

He tensed. "Something happened outside of the car accident and the thing on the roof?"

She sighed and lay her head on his shoulder. "I didn't want to burden you with this."

"I'm your mate, Calita. I know you don't understand fully what that means, but you are essentially my wife. Would you really tell your husband that something this scary to you is not his concern?"

She shook her head after a moment.

"Well thank God, I really thought you were going to say yes. That would've been a problem for me, love. Bears are very protective of their mates, I need you to understand that, and know that everything you are concerned with, concerns me. Am I clear?"

She nodded, a docile bob of her head that appeased both him and his bear. He let it go. He took another deep breath and opened his side of the door and let her crawl out first. He grabbed her bag from the back and left the truck. Intertwining their hands, he was anxious now that they were in his home. He wanted her to like it, hell, to love it. He opened the door in the garage and walked into the mud room, kicking off his shoes. He walked into the kitchen, satisfied at her awe filled gasp.

"Oh my God this kitchen, Simon." She turned a circle, her bare feet soundless on the wooden floors.

"I don't use it, one of my bears, Becca, cooks for me. She showed up to help when my father was sick and has helped me out ever since."

She walked over to the double range and ran her hand over the exposed brick wall behind it. "I love this."

He cleared his throat, "That brick wall was part of the original house my grandfather built."

She whipped around to him, her smile dazzling him. "That's so cool."

Pride bloomed in his chest. "My father sort of rebuilt around the original farm house keeping as much as he could." He pointed up to the exposed wooden beams that stretched from the kitchen through to the living room. "I had those added from the original barn structures."

She rubbed his arm as she passed, padding to his living room. His furniture was large, the cushions deep, and comfortable. Not that he lounged in his bear form, but if he did, the furniture in his house could withstand it. Calita walked over a large painting of the mountains that surrounded his family's land. She traced a light touch over it before turning back to him.

"So you're basically living in your family's history."

She got it. His stomach did a slow tumble, and tension left his shoulders, happy that she loved his space. He bit his tongue. He was seconds from telling her that she could make any changes she needed to make the space hers.

It was way too soon for that.

"Let me show you to the guest room," he said gruffly.

They went up the wide wooden staircase to the upstairs level he'd added to the house. The guest room was the first door at the beginning of the hallway. There was a room closer to his bedroom, but it would be temptation enough with her in his house.

He slid the barn door open and stepped inside the bright room. He set her bag down on the armchair opposite the bed. He kept his eyes anywhere but the small queen-sized bed piled high with pillows and a white down blanket. He hadn't cared how the guestrooms looked, so he'd left the decorating to women in the clan and it showed. The room had a very feminine and airy feel. From his mate's satisfied sigh, they'd done a great job.

Calita put her purse down on the bed. "Thank you. I was…I didn't…"

He grabbed her waist gently and pulled her closer. "I know you need your own space, love."

She raised on her toes and brushed a soft kiss across his lips. "Every time I think I have you figured out."

"Am I supposed to stay away from you while you're here?"

She shook her head, her eyes twinkling. "I didn't say that."

He was thankful. "You have a small bathroom in here, but if you want to take a bath, you'll have to use my bathroom."

She raised an eyebrow.

He put an innocent look on his face. "What? You're going to be sore for a few days. It will be good for you. Come see it, you'll love it."

He took her down the hall, into his bedroom. He showed her into the bathroom and she sighed in feminine pleasure. He wrapped his arms around her from behind.

"Bears like water."

"I can tell," she laughed.

There were two showerheads in the glass enclosed shower and a massive jet tub next to it. "Doesn't that look enticing?"

She snorted and he kissed the side of her neck. "Are you hungry?"

"No."

Her nervousness scented the air still, but she turned in his arms and buried her face in his neck. He rubbed her back. "I can still feel your tension."

She sighed. "I'm a lot more shaken than I want to admit."

He kissed the top of her head. "Let's go look for something sweet in the kitchen. We can settle in and do nothing for the rest of the day."

"That sounds perfect."

– 11 –

Calita rolled over and winced as she pulled her wrist from under her body. Alone in the bed, she lay there waiting until the pain dulled. She glanced at the bedside table and squinted at the time. If was well after eleven. She was a little disappointed at waking up alone, but of course Simon had a ranch to run. He couldn't lay about in bed all day. Though she'd told him she had wanted to sleep alone, in the wee hours of the morning, he'd come into her room, his presence soothing her after the nightmare she'd had.

She stretched, a little less sore than the day before. She knew from experience though, that her wrist would be sensitive for a while. She grimaced. She definitely regretted that she had knowledge of how long bruises and sprains lasted. Nightmares from last night played through her head again, made worst by the fact that she'd been worried about David yesterday. She took a shuddering breath and put it out of her mind.

A bath.

That was what she needed. A good soak, to wash away both the soreness and the residual nightmare. Though, Simon sleeping with her had done that well enough. They'd only slept together a couple nights and she found that she slept so much better when he was in bed with her. Why then had she insisted on a guest room? She sucked her teeth and rolled out of bed. No use examining it.

She padded over to his room and knocked. When no answer or noise sounded, she pushed in. Setting her clothes on the sink, she smiled in anticipation. She piled the bathtub high with the bath salts she found in the cabinet under his sink. As she put them back, she caught a glance at herself in the mirror. Gingerly touching the bandage on her head, she sighed and worked it off. The bruise surrounding the stitches weren't as bad as she thought they'd be, so she chucked the bandage. Minutes later, she sank into the hot water and started the jets. Oh God! She let out a long moan as the water loosened her aching muscles. She closed her eyes and fought to relax. Of course, her mind was going a hundred miles an hour, so she wasn't sure how well that would work.

First thought was of her best friend. She should call Selena and tell her she was okay. But also check to see if she needed help in the restaurant. She snorted. Selena would more than likely tell her off for even asking. She could hear the bossy woman, 'doctor's orders' she'd nag.

Since she'd moved down to Georgia, she and Selena had picked up their friendship right where they'd left off. There was some initial awkwardness as Calita hadn't been sure what her friend would say after so many years apart. Would Selena judge her for the way they parted? Calita had been so wrapped up in David, at his every beck and call and she and Selena had had their fair share of fights over it.

She should've listened to her friend.

She couldn't believe she'd stayed with him as long as she had. Selena warned her that he was too controlling, too volatile, but she'd been in love. And besides, the hitting hadn't really happened until towards the end of their relationship. She'd left after the second time he hit her. Though…that wasn't quite accurate. Calita flexed her sore wrist. There were smaller aggressions she dismissed for months before that. The marks on her skin from where he'd grabbed her. The sprains on her wrists from where he'd bruised the bones after constantly crushing her wrist within his grasp. She'd finally had enough and left him and that night, he'd made sure she paid for it.

Nope, not reliving that.

She surged out of the water, no longer relaxed enough to enjoy it. She quickly dressed in the bathroom and cleaned up after herself. She dropped off her towel and clothes in the guest room and headed downstairs.

There was a woman in the kitchen, humming to herself as she cooked. Jealousy rose and Calita stopped at the end of the stairs, gripping the banister. She forced her fingers off of the wood, one at a time. Simon had mentioned last night that one of his clan women cooked for him. The woman must have sensed her because she looked up. The two of them stared at each other until the other woman broke into a smile.

"Calita, hi. Simon told me to expect you."

Calita returned her smile, if stiffly and walked the rest of the way into the kitchen.

"I'm Becca, I cook for Simon and the ranch hands." Becca extended her hand.

"Simon mentioned that last night, how are you?"

Becca's eyes traced her face, and then down her body, the assessing look curious. "You're certainly different than his ex-wife, that's for sure."

"Excuse me?"

Becca laughed and turned back to her cooking. "Sorry, that was rude. You're the first woman Simon has brought home since his wife, so..."

Calita couldn't figure out whether to be offended or not.

Becca continued with no feedback from her. "That woman was a tiny thing, beautiful, the way most hybrids are. But certainly not built for real country, bear life— not like us."

Calita frowned, trying to figure out if that was, low-key, an insult. She eyed Becca, the woman was tall in the way that most of the bear women in the town were. She hovered over Calita's 5'10 frame, her body thick, solid. But certainly not as big as Calita, weight wise. *The hell did she mean 'built for bear?'*

"It's nice that he's found someone to distract him from thoughts of her." Becca smiled over her shoulder. "Of course, she was in here the other day, but who knows."

Calita didn't like what Becca was insinuating, not because she was self-conscious, but mostly because it didn't sound like Simon at all. He'd come into the restaurant after his ex-wife had left and told a different story than the one Becca told.

"I'd like to take Simon lunch, do you know where he is?" She interjected before Becca could say another word.

The other woman closed her mouth and turned back to the stove. "Umm, well, he keeps a schedule on the chalkboard over there. He likes me to know where he is." She waved vaguely to the wall next to the Subzero refrigerator.

Silence fell in the kitchen and she didn't much feel like breaking it. Becca was nice, but hearing about other women and Simon irritated her. She'd never been possessive, but with him…

Calita discarded the rest of that thought and pulled sandwich fixings out of the refrigerator and set to work. She would not be doing the bitchy girlfriend routine, no matter how peeved she was.

"How long have you worked for Simon?"

Becca paused her stirring. "Well, I started by helping the old Alpha when he fell sick. Simon moved down a few months after I started working here."

Calita made a noncommittal hum.

"Simon brought Miranda, which was his wife, down here with him. She didn't take to country life. She used to be on the 'front lines of the revolution' she would brag. Sickening thing." Becca lowered her voice as though she was telling a secret. "She left Simon not even six months after they'd arrived. I wonder sometimes if he still pines for her."

Since he'd told her differently and in no uncertain terms, Calita merely snorted and continued her task.

"So, how are you finding our town? I heard you're still living in the hotel, have you not made up your mind about staying?"

Calita peeked a look at the woman, but didn't see any malice in her face, just open curiosity.

"I love it here. Complacency more than anything has kept me at the hotel."

Becca nodded and they went back to silence. She wrapped the sandwiches, and hunted down plastic containers in the cabinets. Finding them, she filled them with fruit she found in the fridge and the sandwiches she made. Becca smiled and passed her a picnic basket and blanket. She murmured her thanks and searched the chart for Simon's location.

"It says 'barn work', but we passed like, three different barns when we came here last night."

Becca chuckled. "Simon only cares about his horses, so more than likely he's helping clean their stalls. You can see the barn from the front porch."

Nodding, Calita walked through the living room and out the front door. She sighed as she stepped out into the heat of day. It was a beautiful place. Green manicured grass stretched from the front porch far and wide, divided into different pastures by wooden fences. Becca was right. A large white wooden structure peeked from trees, just past the fence surrounding Simon's house. There was a worn path that lead from the front steps, hopefully to that very building. She meandered down the walkway, her eyes taking in everything. Large trees scattered the property, not including the looming forests surrounding the place. She looked forward to exploring the whole ranch. As she neared closer to the barn her mouth dropped open. The building looked like a church, its size way bigger than she was expecting. The doors were open and rows of horse stalls stretched in front of her.

She spotted Simon in jeans, and shirtless, his curly hair pulled back into a bun. The skin of his chest was glistening with sweat, the jeans riding low enough to make her mouth water. She licked her lips and cradled the basket closer to her chest as if somehow that would keep her heart inside. He sensed her and looked up, their gazes clashing. Her breath stalled and long liquid heat tumbled through her stomach.

He pulled off the gloves he was wearing and closed the distance between them. He smelled of hay, sweat and something else wild and untamed on his skin as he slid his arm around her waist. The kiss he gave her curled her toes and made her dizzy with want. His tongue swept into her mouth, long lazy licks that had her sex throbbing.

"What was that for?" She asked once her senses rushed back.

"Something about my mate on my property just does it for me."

Every time he called her his mate, excitement warred with trepidation in her mind. The more time she spent with him, the more she wanted to belong to him. Caution held her tight, though.

"Isn't this whole town your property?"

His full lips turned up into a smile that made her breathless. "Alpha, though I may be, I don't own the entire town."

She held up the basket with her good wrist. "I brought you lunch, are you able to take a break?"

He nodded and turned to yell for someone to take over what he was doing. He pulled his shirt from his back pocket and pulled it over his head. Her eyes greedily traced his rippling muscles as he worked the shirt on over his sweaty skin.

He lifted the basket out of her hand and grabbed her other one. They started walking, the silence between them comfortable. They approached a lake that was set up with a lifeguard station, and picnic tables as well as lounge chairs. It was a beautiful spot.

"How do you feel about sharing your space with tourists?" His house was visible across the stretch of green grass.

He snorted. "My bears spend way more time here than the tourists do. Tourists come to ride horses and camp. There are some shifters who come to be in their skin without the restrictions most cities put on them, so they keep mostly to themselves. Plus, I dealt with a lot of humans when I lived in Atlanta, I'm used to them."

She pulled out the blanket Becca had given her and spread it on the ground under a big shaded tree. There was a small breeze that blew through the forest behind them. She closed her eyes and lifted her face, enjoying the peace. When she opened them, he was staring at her.

"What?"

"You're so beautiful, you take my breath away."

She swallowed past the lump in her throat and looked away. "You're so sweet."

He grunted, rummaging through the food she'd brought. She looked up as a large guy came up to them. He grunted at Simon and Simon shrugged as he continued to pull out their lunch. They continued their conversation with her looking on in astonishment. There were maybe six actual words intermingled in their discussion. The rest was a series of different sounding grunts. She raised a brow at Simon as the guy lumbered off.

Simon grabbed a hand full of berries and put them in his mouth. He paused when he caught her look. "What?"

"What was that all about?"

He chewed slowly, his brows bunched in confusion. "He asked me if it was okay to allow some of the human teenagers to swim while we're out here."

"And what did you say?"

He shrugged and grabbed a sandwich. "I told him it was up to them if they wanted to keep an eye on humans, I'm on a date."

"You said all that with those grunting sounds you made."

***

Simon chuckled to himself as he realized his mate of course wouldn't understand the communication between bears. "I resent that, there were words mingled in with those grunts."

She snorted, "not very many."

He smiled, loving the exasperated look on her face. "We're bears, darlin', no call for too many words."

She shook her head and smiled, and he stared, transfixed by his mate. She brushed a hand across her bun. He loved the gesture, she made it when she was nervous. He grabbed her hand as she lifted it to do it again. He kissed her palm, inhaling her scent.

"I see you took a bath."

She growled. "Those extra senses of yours are quite annoying."

He laughed and pulled her over to kiss her when he heard a whiz of air moving quickly towards them. Growling, Simon rolled and covered his mate's body as he listened for danger. The thunk of an arrow burying into a tree a scant second later was loud, ominous. The air was still, tension freezing everything around them. Calita moaned and he moved from on top of her.

"Are you okay, love?" his eyes searched the woods around them. There was no movement, even the wind had stilled.

"You landed on my wrist," she whispered, clutching it. "I'm fine otherwise."

He helped her up and reached, snatching the arrow from the tree. He sniffed it, growling at the lack of a distinguishing scent.

"Come, I'm taking you back up to the house while I go figure out who was careless enough to do this."

She looked around, her nervousness dancing throughout her scent. For that alone he would maim whoever had done it. He left their picnic there, rushing Calita down the path to the house. Becca was standing at the front door when they reached it.

She frowned at them. "What happened?"

"Someone shot an arrow at me." Calita answered.

"At you? Are you sure it wasn't an accident?"

"Regardless." Simon growled, shuffling his mate into the house past Becca. He helped her onto a stool at the island and backed away. "I'll be back."

He turned and left, headed towards the barn he'd built to house his offices and a lounge area for the ranch hands. He was pissed. He'd been so full of Calita, and so arrogant that she was safe on his property that he hadn't paid attention to their surroundings. He took full responsibility for even the chance of his mate being harmed. He stormed into the door and found a few of his enforcers and hands sitting around on break, food scattered across the tables.

"Who is in charge of archery today?"

They looked around at each other. One of them stood and glanced at the schedule on the wall. "There is no archery scheduled today."

Simon growled and his bears lowered their head, exposing their necks. He slammed the arrow down on the table.

"This was shot near my mate, and it doesn't carry a scent. I want to know who the hell is shooting on my land without a guide present, and I want to know yesterday."

"Yes, alpha," they scrambled from the barn, all except his beta.

Gavin studied the arrow. "This isn't even one of ours, Alpha."

"I'm aware, Beta. This also isn't the first time my mate has nearly been killed. I want an enforcer on her at all times until I figure this out."

He left the barn, pulling out his cellphone. Nate answered and he explained what happened.

"It's only so far coincidences start to stretch," Nate said after.

"Someone is coming after my mate, Nathan and I want to know who it is. Did you get a chance to check on Miranda and her mate?"

"Of course, Alpha. If we can find proof that it's them, we can kick them out of town without the human authorities getting involved."

Simon growled. "We should kick them out now."

"Yes, well, it seems Charles Rossel has friends in high places. I got a call moments after I typed his name into the law enforcement database. He's got family in government."

He cursed. He hated dealing with the Feds, and avoided it at all cost. Though the humans left them alone generally, they'd written in laws that damn near strangled everything about their culture. Were they living free from human laws, he'd have ran the bear out the moment he saw them. But, the last thing he needed was a complaint launched against his town and an investigation from the oversight committee.

"Fine. I'll stay within the lines."

"Thank ya' kindly," was Nate's response.

Simon ended the call and headed back to his house. Cali was in the kitchen with Becca putting ice on her wrist when he came in. She scowled at him. He smoothed his face, removing all traces of his anger. But as his mate, he was sure Calita could still feel it. He went over to a drawer and pulled out a pad and pencil. He put it on the table next to her. Becca moved, taking the ice with her.

"I want to know everything weird that's been happening to you lately."

"Well, bears are weird, so…" was her cheeky answer.

He grunted, conceding her point.

Her face cleared and she cupped his chin, a smile tilting her lips. It was a grimace really and he assumed she was trying to cheer him up. She ghosted a kiss across his lips and pushed the pad away.

"Did you ever find out who was shooting around the lake?" Calita whispered.

Becca turned around and frowned. "It happened at the lake? There are signs posted, the guests know there's no weapons allowed anywhere near there."

Cali raised her eyebrows. "Well, an arrow shot from across the lake, so obviously not everyone knows."

***

She saw the look exchanged between Becca and Simon. "What am I missing?"

"I'm being overly cautious," Simon murmured, his hands rubbing across her shoulders.

Her heart beat picked up. "You think someone did it on purpose, too?"

Hot scalding fear lurched through her. If she couldn't be safe on Simon's property, then…

He pulled her into his arms. "You're safe here, baby."

She nodded, though not fully believing him.

"Well thank the Creator none of the children were playing there," Becca mentioned.

Oh God, what if one of the clan's kids were hurt because she was around. She stood and rubbed her hands down her shorts. She hadn't thought about bringing danger to someone else. Simon stood with her, shooting Becca a glare.

"Don't worry about that, Cali."

"I'm going to go lay down," she whispered, feeling light headed.

Hours later she was sitting on the bed, barely paying attention to the old rerun on the television. Dinner had been a somber affair. She had a hard time getting out of her own head. The decision of whether she should go back to the hotel kept running through her mind. Would she be safer there? There were ranch hands and bears surrounding this house, logically she would be safer here. If only she could make her mind believe that. She looked up at a tap on the door. Simon leaned against the jamb, his eyes roving her face, studying her.

"Can I come in?"

She nodded and sat up straight, adjusting her gown. He sat on the end of the bed and trailed a hand across the fabric of the duvet.

"So we're still doing the guest room thing?"

She gave him a sheepish smile. "Do you think I'm being silly? We've already had sex, right?"

He shrugged. "I'll do anything to make you feel comfortable, love. Even if it means sneaking in here in the middle of the night to cuddle with you in this little bed instead of the bear sized one I have in my room."

She snorted and hid her face. She sobered a moment later. "I worry what everyone would think, knowing I'm staying here with you."

He gave her a crooked smile and leaned over, nibbling at her lips. "My prudish mate." He stood and walked to the door.

"Goodnight, sweetheart. I'm going to go get some skin time, so don't be alarmed when you hear the doors opening and closing."

"Can I see?"

Wait…what? Had she really asked that? Was it rude? She thought about seeing Marcus transform when he helped her after her accident. Curiosity had her scrambling from the bed. She wanted to see if Simon's bear would scare her.

His eyes widened in surprise, but he nodded. She pulled on a pair of pants under her gown. She followed him outside and he helped her down to sit on the steps. The sounds of the night were all around them, the temperature showcasing the upcoming season change. She was glad she'd put on her pants. Moisture hung in the air and pressed against the skin of her arms. She pulled her legs tight and rested her head on her knees.

He walked a few feet away and she watched with wide eyes as he disrobed. Moisture pooled between her legs, and her heart thumped wildly in her chest as each item of clothing came off. Simon growled low, and Calita squirmed, closing her thighs tightly to still the burn. She licked her lips as his pants cleared his hips and his erection sprang forward. Had she tasted him yet? She would need to rectify that. She gasped as Simon moved quickly, leaning over her, his panting breaths brushing her neck.

"The scent of your arousal is thick in the air, mate."

The deep, gravely timbre of his voice raised goosebumps along her arms. She gripped his dick, and pulled him closer. His eyes had turned nearly gold, his hiss moving the hair on her shoulder. He said nothing as she lowered her body to the next step, putting her face level with his erection. She squeezed her hand, fascinated with the silky feel of the skin surrounding his rock hard shaft. She opened her mouth and moved forward to take him inside. Simon snarled and moved back, leaving her grasping at air.

Biting her bottom lip, she sighed. "I just want a taste."

"Not while I'm already fighting my bear for control." He growled.

"Fine," she pouted.

He laughed, and walked backwards, further away from her. He paused a couple yards away. Fur rippled up and down his skin and his body expanded until a giant nine foot bear stood in Simon's place. Before she could blink, it dropped down to all fours. The bear walked to her, gold eyes glinting in the porch light. It made a chuffing sound and stopped in front of her. She held out a shaking hand, studying its eyes to make sure it was okay. She touched the top of his head and it chuffed again.

She jerked her hand back in surprise.

The bear—Simon, she had to remember it was still Simon— stepped closer and Calita put her hand out again. Simon licked against her skin and she laughed. She rubbed the top of his head and he closed his eyes. He let her play in the rough texture of his fur for long minutes.

"I don't know if you know this, Bear, but Simon blames you for a lot of his impulses," she whispered. A grunt was her answer. "Don't tell him I told you that."

Something that looked like a smile crossed his face. He nuzzled against her skin and then inclined his head towards the house.

"Oh, my time is up?"

The bear's head jerked up, then down.

"I can sit out here and watch you." She wrapped her arms around its massive head, rubbing her cheek against the coarse fur. He pushed against her chest and she laughed. "Fine, I'll go inside."

He gave her one last nuzzle and she stood. Cali paused as she opened the front door and turned around. Simon was watching her. She smiled, touched by the gesture and went to bed.

– *12* –

Dawn's dew had Simon's jeans sticking to his boots, along with grass and hay. He sat at the bench in the mudroom and toed off both boots, frowning as the wet denim flopped against his skin. He'd need to shower and change before the clan started showing up for their clan gathering. Not that they would care if he smelled of horses.

Now that he wasn't busy with the horses, he could admit to himself that he was nervous. It would be Calita's first clan gathering; would the pressure of it push her away? She'd been on his farm for a week, though each day he'd had to convince her to stay another. They'd slept together a couple of those nights, but when she got overwhelmed, Calita would retreat to the guest room.

She was running scared from the mating.

At least, that's what he thought. Simon saw the deliberations on her face when she thought he wasn't looking. It did bode well for him that she was considering it. He just hoped meeting the clan all at once wouldn't backfire and scare her away completely.

He entered the kitchen, silent in socks, pausing as he caught sight of his mate stepping down the last few stairs. She rubbed her eyes, her grogginess evident from her half-closed lids. The short silk pajama shorts she wore rode her thighs with her every step and he clutched the door jamb, his bear surging forward. He cursed the fact that he'd told her no, last night. But his control was tentative at best, especially the way her scent clouded his mind.

By the time he'd wrested control back from his bear, their mate was long sleep.

Staring at her now, he longed to run his hands across the soft skin of her legs. She looked up at him and gave him a sleepy smile. The colorful scarf tied around her hair made her brown skin glow. She stretched and her stomach peeked from beneath her shirt, that tiny strip of skin setting his frozen feet free.

He rushed over to her, lifted her and placed her on the nearest countertop.

She squealed in surprise and wrapped her arms around his neck. "Good morning," she whispered.

"Good morning." He delved into her mouth, tasting her toothpaste and the taste that was all Calita.

She moaned and he deepened the kiss, tilting her chin to get a better angle. He pulled back and was satisfied at the half-hooded gaze she gave him full of heat.

She smiled. "That certainly woke me up."

He chuckled. "The coffee machine is on a timer and should be finished by now, also."

"I definitely still need that."

His eyes devoured her face, cataloguing her every feature. "What are you doing up so early?"

She yawned. "Me? You're up and dressed, so clearly you've been up way before me."

He smiled at her deflection. "Just an hour. This is a functioning ranch. Got a whole list of chores that get done before most people roll over in bed." He traced the dark skin under her eyes. "You didn't sleep well."

He didn't make it a question, he'd heard her tossing and turning all night. The only thing that stopped him from rushing in on her was their agreement. He knew she needed to feel safe, and he imagined barging into her room wouldn't have done that. Though she'd not said anything the other night when he'd done it, he didn't want to push his luck. He swallowed a sigh.

She held his hands in both hers and nuzzled into his palm. "Well, I went to bed horny, so…"

He growled and pulled her hips into his. "You should've stayed up and waited. I had just the cure for that."

"You missed your chance." She snickered. "How did you sleep?"

He smiled, and nipped at her bottom lip. The past few nights she'd been joining him while he got skin time. It had gone much like the first time she'd joined him—with her tempting him past control. The nights before he'd joined her after, but every time they slept together, it was getting harder to stop his bear from claiming their mate. Last night in particular had been…

He adjusted his erection in his pants and pressed against her tight. It had taken him a lot longer last night to calm his bear, hence Calita falling asleep by the time he'd returned to the house.

"Well, my mate insisted on sleeping in the guest room last night again, so my bear complained most of the night."

She traced his clean shaven chin. "I'm sorry."

He grunted. "You don't apologize for that. Just having you under my roof is more than enough."

She nodded. "I told your bear you were blaming him for stuff."

He laughed, a full belly laugh that pulled a smile from her. "You understand that you were talking to me right?"

"I do," she kissed his nose.

He laughed again. "You want to tell me about those nightmares?" He brought the subject back around.

She was saved by Becca coming into the door. He snarled at the female and Becca rolled her eyes.

"Well, good morning, Alpha. Calita." Becca dropped the small grocery bag she was carrying on another counter.

"Good morning," Calita waved.

"The clan will be here in a few hours, and I want to shower before they arrive." He nuzzled into his mate's neck. "Want to join me?" He whispered.

Calita gripped his chin and stared into his eyes, giving him a subtle nod.

A purr rocked through his chest and he lifted his mate from the counter. Was it rude to leave? Probably. But did his bear care when the prospect of being inside their mate loomed.

Hell no.

"Put me down," Calita hissed as he climbed the stairs with her. "I'm too big for you to carry like this."

He kissed her to stop her fussing, their tongues dueling the whole way up the stairs. He set her down once they reached his bathroom. He stared into her eyes, gauging her comfort.

"Are you sure, love?" He pulled his t-shirt from his jeans.

Calita licked her lips. "Absolutely."

"No more shyness, I've seen your scars," he whispered against her lips.

She took a shuddering breath, their air mingling. He thought she would back down but she nodded and reached for the hem of her tank top. Lord above, his mate was going to get naked in front of him. He didn't realize how much he wanted that. His bear reared the moment the silk camisole cleared her breasts. Simon stepped forward and cupped the heavy weight of them, his rough palm grazing her warm skin. She sucked in a breath, as he trailed over her nipples. His hands roamed down the skin of her rounded stomach, his touch light as they breezed back up.

He traced the skin of her chest, drifting down to the scars that she would always carry. She was so strong, his mate. In ways she would never consider. She didn't flinch as his hand moved over one of the razor thin scars bisecting right beneath her breasts. His bear shuddered, his power saturating the bathroom as he thought about everything she'd been through. He looked up and her vulnerable gaze speared him.

"My beautiful, strong mate," he growled before devouring her mouth.

Her body trembled beneath his hands. He sipped at her lips, taking in her every sigh as her body relaxed. Finally her hands wrapped around his neck and she arched in his arms.

"There you are," he whispered against her lips.

He backed them up until they reached the shower stall, pausing only to start the water. She pulled at his shirt and he tossed it aside. She kissed his shoulders as he stepped out of his pants. He pushed down her shorts with impatient hands, helping her step out of them. He growled and pulled her into the shower stall. Hot water pelted his back, but he didn't release his mate's lips. Their tongues dueled, desperation adding heat to their caresses. He pressed her into the cold tile, lifting one of her legs around his waist.

"Yes," she hissed, arching.

He leaned down and sucked a nipple, laving it, his teeth grazing across it. He trailed his hands down to her sex and found her wet and wanting.

"Ready for me, love?"

She nodded, her eyes meeting his, need broadcasting clear. He circled his shaft at her entrance and took a deep breath. Giddy, his hands shook as he guided himself back to her center. He loved the feel of her. He pushed in, closing his eyes as the walls of her sex gripped his cock. He let out a rough exhalation, forcing his body still so he could bask in the feel of her body.

***

Calita squirmed and he pulled back, his hips working as he pushed back in. For every thrust inside, her body tightened, building on an orgasm she wasn't quite sure she was ready for. Simon didn't rush, his strokes were slow, sensual thrusts that stalled her breath. Her womb clenched and she arched her back, wanting to take in his every inch.

She gripped his ass, pulling him into her body, grinding her clit against him on his every push in. Steam built in the shower stall, beading against their skin. She licked at his shoulder, sucking on the skin of his neck. His hips jerked and he growled when her teeth scraped against the front of his neck.

"Careful, love, you're not ready for what that brings." His eyes were gold, a savage need shining through them.

He might be right.

Simon picked up his speed, and her nails gripped his shoulders. Her legs shook, and heat gathered in the pit of her stomach, spreading to her sex. Simon reached between them and plucked at her clit, sending her reeling. The orgasm burst throughout her body, potent in its intensity. Tension flowed from her body, but an exhilarating wave of heat rushed back in until she was dizzy. His hips stiffened as he drove in once more, his body shuddering, growls rumbling his chest as he came. She tightened her leg around his waist and rode out the orgasm, a languid smile tipping up her lips.

Oh God, she felt amazing. Revitalized. Instead of sleeping, she wanted to shower and go down to his amazing kitchen and play with dough. Her mind was clear, the fog she'd lived with for years, gone.

Simon growled in her ear before nipping the skin underneath. "I can feel your happiness."

She hummed in answer. He chuckled and pulled from her. His kiss was slow, lazy after the frantic pace of their sex. They took turns showering each other, their hands playful, and the kisses leisurely. Her mood was buoyed, her steps light as she left his bathroom to change.

Less than an hour later, Calita came down in a long comfortable skirt and a loose white tank top. She wasn't sure of the dress code for clan day, but she figured since it would be outside, she wanted to be comfortable. Becca was cutting vegetables near the sink. She gave Calita a cursory glance and went back to her task.

"Is there anything I can do to help?"

"It's sort of a potluck, so you can make anything you'd like to."

That made perfect sense with the amount of bears she was sure would attend. She wandered around the kitchen to see what type of ingredients Simon, or rather Becca, kept in the kitchen. She knew the bears all had a sweet tooth, a couple easy to make desserts would be her contribution. All of the ingredients were there, so Calita got started. She and Becca worked in silence. It wasn't weighted, not so far as she could tell, so she relaxed and enjoyed the quiet. She was an only child, silence never bothered her.

"I love this kitchen so much," Calita said more to herself as she started the mixer. "I imagine you're responsible for all the appliances being in here."

Becca snorted. "If it were up to Simon, or any of the enforcers for that matter, this kitchen would be full of barbecue spices and frozen foods."

"Hey, I resent that," Simon said as he entered the kitchen. He kissed the side of Calita's neck.

Her body hummed and she wished they were alone. "Are you here to help cook?"

"Well…"

She chuckled as she finished the batter for the cakes. Despite his reluctance, he did give her a hand. More to say, he tasted batter and icing while she worked. She rolled her eyes as she turned and caught him sticking another spoon into her icing. She popped his hand.

"Stop that," Calita chided.

He growled and lifted her. She squealed as he tried to take her from the kitchen.

"You have guests!" She giggled.

He turned towards the front door as they heard the sounds of vehicle doors opening and closing. "Saved by my bears."

Waves of women entered his house moments later, bringing their noise with them. They were carrying trays of food, with male bears behind them carrying the heavier containers. Calita watched from the refrigerator where Simon had deposited her and stayed out of their way since she didn't have anything else to do. She waved as some of the women greeted her with more than a few curious looks.

"Calita," Selena greeted her with a huge hug. "Are you okay, is Simon treating you okay?"

Conversation paused and all eyes turned to them.

"You're staying here?" One of the older women asked.

"Of course, the Alpha would want to make sure his mate was okay after the accident." Another chimed in.

"You poor thing," A woman came and guided her into a chair at the island. "You shouldn't be up. There are enough hands around here to help."

"Well, I've already made rolls and a cake, all that's left to do is glaze them." She pointed to the oven timer.

"I can help, grandmother." Anna, the young woman who'd been helping her in Selena's kitchen volunteered.

Calita smiled. She waved, happy to see her. "I'm perfectly capable of doing it."

Selena passed her a knife and a bag of oranges with a grin. "Alpha said you had to take it easy."

"Oh lord, demoted to prep," Calita said with a smile. She shot Simon a fake look of irritation.

He held his hands up and left the house, a grin on his face.

Her best friend chuckled, but then sobered. "Simon called Nate the other day. He's looking into the problem you had, you know at the lake…and the others."

"What problems, what's happening?" Anna's grandmother eyed her sharply.

"Someone shot an arrow at Calita," Becca said from across the kitchen.

Gasps sounded, the women turning to her in sympathy.

Anna frowned from the stove. "Becca, don't you teach the archery classes?"

"That's the thing, there were no archery classes yesterday," Becca shrugged.

Jerica rubbed her shoulder as she passed. "Well, that's just bizarre."

The conversation went back to town gossip and Calita's shoulders relaxed. She enjoyed being in the middle of the women, their conversation comforting her. But, she was thankful not to have their undivided focus.

"Calita, are your parents still in Chicago?" Charmaine asked.

The question brought her out of her daydream. "Yes. They both teach at the local college there."

Some of the older women nodded in approval and went back to their discussion. Soon they were calling for some of the men to come in and pick up the trays. She lifted a tray of cookies and winced.

"Put that down." Selena was at her shoulder fussing. "Relax, you aren't supposed to be doing anything strenuous."

"Nothing strenuous? Staying in this house with her m—"

Selena pushed a young woman out of the kitchen before she could finish that sentence.

***

Simon hefted one of the picnic tables closer to the others per instructions of his great aunt who watched from a chair in the shade. She directed the men, her sharp orders contrasting the loving looks she gave the children playing around her. Simon smiled, the sight of the children relaxing his bear. He'd found his mate, and it wouldn't be long before his child was in the midst of the playing children. His heart pitched, longing stealing his breath. Did Calita even want children? He wasn't sure, but imagining her swelling with his cub choked him up.

He was looking around when he spotted Nate walking up.

He met him halfway across the yard. "What did you find?"

Nate stuffed his hands in the pocket of his jeans. "We're still looking into the car, but nothing so far."

Simon growled.

"I did look into one Charles Moses Rossel."

"And?"

Nate raised his eyebrows. "It's like I said, two minutes after hitting send on the search, I got a call from an… interested government party."

"Shit." Simon folded his arms over his chest. Exactly what he didn't want.

"Yeah, seems Charles has contacts in some high places. I was questioned sly like to find out what I wanted. I told him I was doing a potential resident check."

"And what did they say?"

"That I'd done enough digging on the matter and if there were any further questions my alpha should contact them." Nate's smirk came and went in a tiny second.

"Exactly what the hell I didn't want," he muttered.

"In other news, I did go up on the roof. The moorings around the satellite dish were definitely tampered with. There was weathering except where the lines were cut. I had the guys take prints, there was nothing."

Simon hissed in anger, turning to get his bear under control. For a day that had started with such potential, it was going to hell in a handbasket quickly. Nate waited him out, his face placid, calm as it always was by the time Simon turned back around.

"Tell me more about what happened the other day."

Simon growled. "An arrow came at Calita."

Nate rubbed the back of his neck. "Where was she?"

"At the lake, eating lunch with me."

Nate grunted. "Y'all kept the arrow?"

"Of course."

"I'll get it from Gavin and add it to the list. I don't believe in coincidences, Cousin."

"Neither do I, Nathan. I told Miranda to leave, but she and Charles keep popping up places. Think he could have anything to do with it? Their scent was on the property the other day, but it was old."

"Hmm," Nate stared off in the distance. "Let me go make some calls."

"Alpha." One of his enforcers came up to them. "I have the perimeter secure, and I set a few men around the lake to further secure our clan gathering."

He nodded and turned his attention back to Nate. "It can wait until after the clan gathering."

Nate nodded and left to help the women filing out of the house. Simon spotted his mate standing and helping the women set up the food. He caught her wince and rushed to her side.

"Calita," his growl brought her head up. "Why aren't you sitting and taking it easy?"

"I'm not lifting anything."

Her pout caught him off guard and stuck a pin in his anger. His chest deflated, the next argument releasing as a sigh from his lips.

"Baby, sit, please." He guided her over to a bench near where the women were still setting up so she wouldn't be isolated.

Her hands were shaking as she pushed her hair behind her ears. It wasn't in its usual bun on the back of her head. The strands were ruffling with the slow wind moving through their lake. He leaned down and kissed the pout from her mouth.

"Please rest, and take it easy. There are enough people here to do what's needed."

"Is what we did in the shower earlier what you'd consider rest?" Her eyes sparked with temper.

The visual of what they'd done in the shower had saliva pooling in his mouth. He clenched his teeth rather than admit to her point.

"Hmm, that's what I thought." She leaned closer, "if you don't object to that, then you have no leg to stand on regarding this."

She had a point, but damn if it didn't piss his bear off. A growl rattled his chest and he leaned over his mate.

"Alpha," the radio at his hip sounded.

He stared into his mate's eyes until she dropped her gaze. She was holding his eyes a little longer…good. Despite her misgivings about their mating, her body and subconscious were already going through the changes to become his.

Fucking right.

He pulled the radio off his belt. "Go ahead."

"Got a disturbance, west gate."

He snarled at the interruption. He leaned further into Calita's space. "We'll be discussing this later, mate."

Her eyes widened and the pulse at her neck skittered. He backed away quickly before he dragged her back to the house.

– *13* –

Calita watched Simon leave, breathless with want. How he managed to rile both her temper and her lust confused her. She turned away from his retreating backside and got up to finish helping the women. She found them all staring at her.

"What?"

One of the older women snorted. "Had he not been interrupted, he would've pulled you away for a 'talking to'."

Calita frowned at the air quotes. "What does that mean?"

Giggles met her question. Selena touched her shoulder. "Most of the male bears have this dominance game they like to play with their mates."

"It ain't a game for some." Someone chimed in, and a chorus of raucous laughter erupted.

"Dominance?" Calita asked.

"They like their women submissive," Anna supplied.

She thought on the fact that Simon had promised to let her have control of their relationship. She looked at her best friend and Selena shrugged. She knew damn well Selena was nowhere near submissive, so maybe it wasn't something Simon needed?

"The males try to find any reason to punish their mates." A woman said fanning her face.

"The punishments are the best part about arguing with your mate. I purposely set off his bear sometimes." An older woman said with a wink.

High fives went around.

She wanted to ask the woman to elaborate, but the conversation had gone on far enough as far as she was concerned.

"Do you know what that was about?" Selena pulled her attention.

"What, Simon leaving?"

Selena nodded.

Cali cleared her throat. "I don't."

"So, Calita, has Simon talked to you about the duties of the alpha female?" Anna's grandmother asked.

Becca choked at the same time she did.

Calita's eyes widened. "Well, see, we ummm…"

One of the kids started crying and all eyes swiveled, their attention diverted.

"I um…I'm going to use the restroom."

Selena snickered as she stood quickly and rushed towards the house.

***

Simon trotted over to where two of his enforcers stood around a saw horse. It wasn't much in the way of a deterrent, but it wasn't really meant to be one. Normally no one guarded it, but with the accidents happening to Calita, he wasn't taking any chances. Gavin met him coming through from the other side of the forest. Simon frowned, wondering why his Beta had been called. He spotted Miranda and Charles, a moment later and growled. His ex-wife was nothing if not persistent.

"What are you doing here?" He didn't address Miranda, but her companion.

"Well, I heard there was a bear gathering, I thought I would check it out."

"There are no outsiders allowed in," Marcus, his enforcer, said firmly. "I've explained it to him already, Alpha."

"Miranda's not one for hearing no a lot, so I'm not surprised you had to say it more than once."

Charles' eyebrows lowered, his shoulder hunched over, the hair on his neck visibly bristling. Jealous rage wafted off the other bear a moment before Charles tamped it down. Simon narrowed his eyes, further curious as to why the male was adamant about being on his clan's land. Was it his property, or access to Simon's bears the two were seeking? Miranda had claimed to need a safe space, but their desperation told a different story.

Simon crossed his arms over his chest. "We don't allow outsiders into our gathering."

"That's not welcoming at all," came Charles's rumbling answer. "I would think you'd want to invite a fellow bear to commune with the clan."

Yeah, it was access to his bears. Were the two of them recruiting? Recruiting for a war long done? There were shifters from certain sectors that hadn't wanted to negotiate at all with the humans, and saw the treaty between the two as nothing more than a stalling tactic. Was Miranda still caught up in it? He thought about the young cubs in his clan. The call to revolution would be tempting to some, but he kept his bears happy enough that hopefully, he wouldn't have to worry about them. But to be safe, he'd keep Charles from mingling with his bears.

Simon let his bear come to the surface a little. His shoulders expanded in size, fur sliding out of his skin. "This is an all-inclusive ranch. There are bears aplenty on the property if you need to commune, but this gathering is for clan only. Had you come onto my land correctly, and not skulking, you'd have been apprised of that fact." His bear rumbled his chest and power flooded his body, mingling with the anger already there. A dangerous combination.

He stepped closer to Charles and Miranda. "You've now been on my land for more than a week without filing the proper permissions. That ends today. I'll have someone escort you from the property. You have twenty-four hours to leave my county. If I find you here again, I'll assume that means you want to challenge my clan and we'll set it up." Simon inclined his head to his beta and knew that Gavin would get it done.

He texted Nate as he left, apprising him of the situation. If it came down to it, he'd have to go through the sheriff's office to kick Miranda and her mate out of town. He walked past his house to get to the picnic area and smiled as his mate came out of the front door of his house. Calita looked up, seeming to sense him. She gave him an awkward smile. He thought back to their earlier disagreement, was she still mad? He held out his hand as he got closer.

"Walk with me?"

She grabbed his hand and they walked in silence, trekking through the forest. The dense trees provided shade, dampening some of the day's heat.

"What's on your mind, Cali?"

She sighed. "I just...this is awkward."

He raised an eyebrow, "our walking?"

She shook her head, biting her lip. She struggled with the words; they flitted across her mind as she turned to look at him.

He lifted her hand and kissed her knuckles. "Tell me, darling."

"The women were talking, you know, about mates." She turned her head away from him.

He stopped walking and used her chin to bring her back around to face him. "What is it?"

Her shoulders slumped. "They said bears are into dominance and submission games."

"Yes?" He prodded.

"Well, am I holding you back? You know, with how we are in bed."

He was confused by what was worrying her. "Do you imagine I have complaints about our sex life?"

"I just…" she growled. "I know you said I could control everything, but I don't want to deprive you of something your bear needs."

He'd been worried that the women would say something that would upset her, but he'd never imagined sex coming up. "What did I tell you when we started?"

She looked up at him, her eyes luminous with unshed tears. Why was she working herself up over it? He didn't understand.

"I told you I was direct, yes?"

She nodded.

"Have I lied to you about anything, sweetheart? I would tell you if there was a problem."

She let out a relieved breath. "You're right. I'm sorry, I just got a little insecure."

He leaned his forehead against hers. "Don't apologize for your feelings. I want you to come to me when you have a concern."

She nodded. He kissed her, cradling her face in his hands. She gripped his wrists and opened her mouth. Their tongues tangled and she melded their bodies together.

"Now, let's talk about how you're depriving me."

Her eyes widened until she realized he was teasing. She swatted his chest. "That's not funny."

"It's quite a serious matter," he joked, lifting her skirt.

She looked around. "Simon, we can't," she whispered.

He tsked and fondled her breasts through the thin top she wore. "You would deprive your mate?" He bent down and pulled one of the small buds into his mouth.

She hissed. "Not fair."

He backed her up against the nearest tree. "No?" His fingers delved underneath her underwear. "I don't know anything about fair, but damn woman you feel amazing." He pulled his fingers up to his lips and slipped them in his mouth, closing his eyes at her taste.

"Simon," she whispered.

"Yes, my love?" He crowded her. He unzipped his pants, freeing his erection.

She moaned as he rubbed against her wet cleft. Lifting her and wrapping her legs around his waist, he paused until she gave him her eyes.

"There you are," he whispered, "I want you, here, now, yes or no, darling?"

She nodded, her face flushed.

He rubbed their cheeks together, reveling in her soft skin. "Words, my mate."

"Yes," she whispered.

He took her lips in a scorching kiss, entering her in one stroke. He wanted to make sure she would never question their sex again. He kept his strokes slow, aware that her ribs had to still be aching, enjoying her pants of pleasure. He closed his eyes as she squeezed around him. Her fingers tightened in his hair, and she nipped at his neck. His bear responded immediately, power flooding his body.

"Careful, Cali," he warned, his speed picking up.

She whimpered and her sex gripped him tightly. Gods, the feel of her. He took her mouth again, the slow sensual duel of their tongues raising goosebumps along his arms. He had to find a way to show her how much she meant to him. She pulled back and gasped, tensing as she exploded. He followed behind her, his body bowing under the onslaught of pleasure.

It took him long moments to catch his breath. He pulled out and lowered her gently, sipping at her lips as she sighed. He used her panties to clean her off and tucked them into his jeans pocket, hiding his smug smile. Her eyes finally drifted open, a satisfied smile tipping her lips.

"Okay, I believe you."

He laughed and draped his arm around her shoulder, leading them back to the party.

"I feel like everyone knows what we did," she whispered as they entered the clearing.

He kissed her neck, hiding his smile at his prudish mate. He would keep the bit of news that they more than likely would smell the scent of sex on them.

For the rest of the evening, he watched as Cali interacted with his clan, pride and a sense of belonging flowing through him. He was one step closer to claiming her as his own.

– 14 –

The smell of coffee and cooking meat greeted her as she came downstairs. She slept in Simon's bed last night, and had awakened this morning feeling a lot better. She rotated her wrist as she padded into the kitchen. There was still pain when she moved it, but nothing she couldn't handle. Becca was humming at the stove. Calita greeted her as she fixed herself a cup of coffee. She rolled her neck and debated what she would do today. Last night with Simon had her seriously considering his offer.

He called her his mate, and staying in his house, sleeping in his bed, she was starting to feel like it. Yesterday, hanging out with the clan was comfortable. Both men and women treated her as though she belonged already. She felt welcomed. She'd been holding herself back from the town and its residents, yesterday had changed that. Regardless of her outcome with Simon, she would stay here.

"Did you enjoy the clan gathering?" Becca broke into her thoughts.

"Funny, I was just thinking about it. I had a great time."

Becca hummed. "That's awesome. I'm glad nothing happened. I was worried, what with your accidents and all."

"Yeah, thank God," she murmured into her cup.

The sound of the door opening and stomping feet proceeded Simon entering the kitchen. He smiled when he spotted her, making a beeline for her.

He grabbed her waist and leaned over her mouth. "I loved waking up with you in my bed," he murmured against her lips.

She snorted. "I'm sure it helps that you get morning sex, which, don't get used to that."

He laughed and she was fascinated with him.

"What are you doing today?" He sipped at her lips.

She leaned back. "Well, I want to go into work and see if Selena needs help."

His gaze pinned her and she fought not to squirm. He said nothing for a long moment. Was he formulating an argument? After a moment of silence, he sighed.

"You'll take it easy?"

She nodded quickly.

"Cali," he growled, "you're still injured, and the doctor said at least two weeks, so you will be careful." He grabbed her chin and made her look into his eyes.

She wasn't scared, points for her. She kissed him. "I promise, I won't lift anything heavy, I'll just hover."

He grunted and kissed her. "Ok. There are keys in the garage. You can take either of the cars."

She bit her lip and debated changing her mind. She wasn't quite ready to get behind the wheel of a car.

"Would you prefer someone drive you?"

She let out a breath and felt like a coward. "Yeah, I didn't drive much in Chicago, so the accident really shook me up."

He walked over to the phone on the wall and pushed a button. A few minutes later a large bear of a man came into the kitchen. He greeted Becca and then smiled at Calita.

"Cali, this is Zeke, he will be your personal chauffer today," Simon introduced him.

"Oh, you don't have to do that, you can just drop me off."

There was something in Simon's expression as he smiled. "Zeke will hang out with you today, in case you need anything."

Simon's face was smug as though she'd given him some kind of concession. What had she missed? She nodded, deciding to ignore it for now. She gave him a quick kiss and headed to get dressed.

***

Simon waited until he heard the door close in the guest room and he turned to Zeke. "You're with her all day."

"Yes, Alpha, I'll keep her safe," Zeke assured him.

Simon breathed out in relief and sat down to breakfast. Cali came downstairs thirty minutes later in jeans and a simple vee neck, her hair back in its customary bun.

She leaned down and kissed him. "See you later?"

"I'll be here when you get back." He gave her a lingering kiss and waved as she and Zeke headed to the garage.

A few moments later there was a knock on his back door. He stood and allowed entrance for one of the elder males in the clan.

"Elder Bishop, good morning. Would you like some coffee?" Becca reached to pull down a mug.

"No, thank you. Alpha, if I could have a moment of your time."

"Of course, *kamassa'*. We can go into the office." Simon led the elder into his downstairs office.

It was neat as a pin seeing as how he rarely used it. He had an office in the barn the other ranch hands used as a lounge. Curiosity had him watching the elder as he walked around to his desk. The *kamassa'*, or elders, in their clan were the older bears that had once held high ranking enforcer positions. He had the utmost respect for them all. He gestured for Bishop to sit, waiting until the male was seated before he took his own chair. His bear knew that despite age, the male was still strong.

"What can I help you with, Bishop?"

"There's something going on in this clan," Bishop spoke after a moment.

"Something I'm unaware of?" Simon asked, sitting up in his chair and bracing his elbows on the desk.

"Your mate has been in how many accidents?"

Simon growled as frustration filled him. He knew what the Elder Bishop was insinuating. The longer he let the attacks on Calita happen without resolution, the more it undermined his position.

"You've led this clan with firm and fair leadership. We've thrived under you, Simon, so understand that I don't come to you with admonishments, but concerns. There is someone spreading that you are unable to keep your mate safe."

His growl bounced off the walls of his office, his bear battering against his skull.

The elder held up his hand. "The rumors are being dismissed as soon as the lie is brought forward, but it doesn't negate that someone is making a concentrated effort to keep the rumor moving. You know how this town is. While the bears are taking care to squash the talk, the humans have no concept of the trouble they're spreading."

He sighed and wiped a hand across his face. If word that the alpha was having issues protecting his mate left the confines of this town, there was no telling what type of trouble would show up just to see if it was true. He had no desire to have challenges working through his clan.

"Anything else?"

The elder shook his head.

"I'll take care of it."

"Of that I have no doubt, Alpha."

***

Calita guided Zeke into one of the parking spots behind the diner, wanting to slip in without any of the customers seeing. The last thing she wanted to do was answer questions. She'd answered a lot last night at the clan gathering, and she was done feeding gossip. She opened the door and the sounds that greeted her immediately relaxed her shoulders. The sizzling of the grills, the low hum of the machines and ribald conversation flowing were all music to her ears.

The smells were the next thing to hit her. Cooking meats, baked bread and the fresh, bright scent of chopped vegetables greeted her. She smiled. She'd missed being in the kitchen. Selena pushed through the swinging door from the dining room and pointed her finger at Calita.

"You're not supposed to be in here for another few days."

Cali waved away her friend's concern. "You know I can't sit around."

"You're supposed to be resting, Calita. Not to mention with everything else going on. Won't you feel better at Simon's, under—"

"Under what?" Calita raised her eyebrow.

Selena cleared her throat. "Simon can protect you better at the ranch."

"I was almost shot with an arrow at the ranch, you sure about that?"

Selena looked around nervously and raised her voice a little, "I trust the alpha."

Activity in the kitchen slowed, the volume lowering as some leaned in to hear their conversation.

"I trust Simon to keep me safe, Selena, that's not what I meant."

Her friend's shoulders slumped in relief and the vibe in the kitchen relaxed along with her.

"What is that about?" She whispered, looking around.

Selena pulled her further away from the others in the kitchen. "Rumors are flying and it's not healthy for the clan to have doubt in their alpha."

She peeked behind Selena's back and the staff hastily went back to cooking and cleaning. There were so many intricate details involved in dealing with the bears. Could she handle being Simon's mate, knowing that would make her alpha female?

"I just needed to be back in the kitchen."

"No."

Cali sighed. "Selena."

"No."

She stared at her friend and put on her most pitiful pout. Selena growled and held up her hands. "Fine. You can watch and bark from that table in the corner." She pointed to the table, she and Simon had sat at days ago. "Zeke, you want something to eat?"

He smiled, "always Selena."

She smiled and walked off.

Cali went over to the table with Zeke, barking at a couple of the cooks as she passed them. They scrambled to do her bidding and she smiled. Okay, she couldn't work, but she could still have fun.

– *15* –

Calita was smiling hours later as Zeke dropped her off at the house. She entered the kitchen intending to cook for Simon. She would put up candles on the table, if she could find them, really set the mood for a date. She sighed as the smell of dinner cooking reached her in the mudroom. Not that she had anything against Becca helping Simon, but she didn't like the idea of another woman cooking for Simon. Did that make her a jealous person?

Probably.

She walked into the kitchen in her socks. "Becca, while I'm here, you don't have to cook for Simon. I can handle it." She kept her voice neutral.

Still, the look Becca gave her showed the other woman's irritation. "It's my job, and has been for years, don't worry about it. You should relax while you're here."

Rather than confronting the woman—who she was starting to feel was a little too familiar with Simon—Calita decided it would be better to leave the kitchen. She'd brought dessert from Selena's, barking at Anna to make it just right. The young woman was turning out to be an excellent assistant. She followed directions well, learned fast as hell, and put up with Calita with an easy smile. She liked her. She had plans, and the more she got involved with Simon, the more elaborate her plans became. Anna would make an easy addition to those plans.

She looked at Becca again, stirring at the stove and sighed. She put the dish down on the counter. "I'm going for a walk," she said over her shoulder.

The land was beautiful, the surrounding trees peaceful. A year into this town and she was starting to feel at home. She wondered how much Simon had to do with that. She finally felt comfortable enough to look for her own place and the small idea she'd had about opening a bakery was starting to feel real. Could she do it? There was nothing stopping her. There wasn't one in town, and the one in Pleasant Hill wasn't half as good as her, and that wasn't bragging, that was directly out of the mouths of the bears who came into Selena's diner. She could certainly do it. Excitement started to fill her. She wrapped her arms around her waist as darkness started to fall.

She looked around and realized she'd been walking a lot longer than she'd planned to, and had gone a lot further. She bit her lip and her good mood plummeted as panic threatened to rear up. Where was she? She turned in a circle, the trees all looking the same. She should be able to just turn around and walk back the way she came. Easy, right? She looked up, and tried to see if she could spot any of the barn structures from the trees. She shivered half an hour later as she realized it wasn't easy. She cursed her foolishness for leaving without her cellphone. Was she even still on the ranch? Shouldn't there be flat land, grazing pastures or something that would give her some kind of bearing? She spotted a small cabin through the woods and decided to get help there. Simon had told her that tourists rented the places, shifters and humans alike. She could use their phone to call the ranch.

There was a man and woman standing on the porch watching her as she got closer. The man came down and smiled.

"Lost?"

"Just a little, I was hoping to use your phone to call to the main house." She stopped walking, some instinct giving her pause as the man stepped into the light.

"Sure, come on in." Light glinted off his pupils, giving his eyes a sinister glow.

Not just a man then, a shifter. She didn't move, her mind telling her to run in the other direction, her body momentarily defying the logic of that instinct. The man stepped closer and snapped her out of her momentary stupor.

"That's okay, actually, I can find my way back."

She walked backwards, not wanting to put her back to the stranger. The conversation she'd had with Simon about how fast bears moved, darted through her mind. She couldn't be sure he was a bear shifter, but it was safe to say she couldn't outrun any shifter.

That point was brought home quickly as he moved, his hand gripping her neck, claws resting right against her skin before she could blink.

"No, I insist," he snarled.

He grabbed her around the waist and she kicked, fighting to get from his grip. She made her body limp, but he scooped her up, her dead weight no deterrence. Calita kicked, screaming, scratching at his face. Still, he overpowered her. She gave a single glance to the woman watching from the porch, praying she would intervene. The woman simply crossed her arms over her chest, as though bored. The man continued towards the cabin, but then tensed, pausing, his head cocked to the side. Calita used the break to renew her escape attempt. The sound of her name being called reached her and she screamed out.

"I'm here!"

The man dropped her and she hit the ground hard, the wind being knocked from her body, her ribs throbbing anew. She rolled over as Zeke came through the trees. Simon wasn't far behind him, scooping her into his arms.

"What are you doing out this far?" He barked.

Tears crested her eyes as she bent her wrist. "I didn't mean to walk so far. Some guy was here and he tried to drag me into that cabin."

He stilled, taking a deep inhale. A growl left his throat. "I don't smell anyone on you. Zeke." He inclined his head towards the woods.

Zeke took off at an alarming speed, changing mid run into a large black bear. Simon growled again and turned and walked her back into the woods from where he'd come. They came out on the other side, a battered black truck still running, with both doors open. He put her down on her feet outside of the truck.

"What happened?"

"I just wanted to walk before dinner and I got turned around. I saw a cabin and was going to ask the people inside if I could use their phone, you said the ranch was safe."

"Calita, you're no longer on the ranch," he growled. "Get in the truck."

She flinched, but quickly did as he said. She hauled her body into the big truck and closed the door. Simon stalked across the front of the truck, the headlights reflecting off his features. His face was angry, the cheekbones standing out, his dark eyes glinting. She tensed when he opened the door. He was pissed, that much was evident. He didn't say anything, simply slammed the door closed and took off. She grabbed the bar above the window and sucked in a breath.

She watched the scenery as they drove back to the main house and her heart thudded as she realized how far she'd gone.

Calita was used to walking every afternoon, used to making a circle around town, and in her musings she'd not realized how far from the house she'd gone. She shuddered, still remembering the feel of the stranger's claws at her neck. She snuck a glance at Simon and saw his jaw flexing, his eyebrows lowered in vexation. It brought back memories of David and for a moment fear rose in her. Anytime David was as angry as Simon appeared to be, the night would end badly for her. She slid closer the door, gripping the bar tight to still her trembles.

Rumbling sounds vibrated in the car as they pulled up home, his temper still roused. She reached for the door. Simon had said before that he liked taking care of her, so she paused with her hand on the knob. When David was in a mood like the one Simon was in, it was best to do everything as right as possible. She dropped her hand into her lap and waited on him. He came around the truck and opened the door. He reached for her and she barely, by a hair, kept from flinching. His eyes went flinty, hard, and she knew she was making him madder.

He lifted her from the truck, his touch gentle, careful with her as he gripped her waist. He gently set her feet on the ground, holding on until she got her footing.

He nodded towards the house. "Go on ahead, I need to put the truck away and take care of a few things."

He was pissed and she wavered between her instinct to run as fast as she could up the porch, or to turn and soothe him, hoping to lessen his anger. She tensed, unsure what to do.

He closed his eyes, his body visibly trembling. He took a shuddering breath. "Please, Calita, go on inside the house, I can't leave until I'm sure you're safe inside."

She gave him a jerky nod and quickly rushed into the house. Conflicted. He was upset, with her especially it seemed, but he wasn't treating her any different than he would normally. She grabbed her purse from the kitchen counter and went upstairs. She wanted her phone near her just in case. *Just in case…what?* That thought stopped her. She paused at the top of the stairs and stared at his bedroom door. Did she wait for him in his room or hide in her own? Hiding had never helped her before. She turned to Simon's room and paused at the door. She took several panicked breaths, until Simon's scent filled her and for some reason calmed her slightly. It slid through the panic and she remembered that Simon had at no point given her a reason to fear for her safety with him. She promised herself when she'd moved to Bear Ridge she would be a different person here. She sighed and with still some trepidation, went into his room.

***

Simon was pissed. He should've smelled whoever touched his mate and he hadn't, which meant the bastard, whoever it was, was using some type of scent blocker. How the fuck was the bear getting near his land without his enforcers knowing? Tourists brought strange smells with them all the time, and there was a lot of land to cover, but, even knowing it was hard to cover every corner, he was pissed.

He had to admit, a good portion of his anger stemmed from his mate's reaction to him. Calita had flinched from him. FLINCHED! Her first instinct to prepare her body for a blow. He wanted to tear shit up just thinking about it. The thought of her being hurt on his property, of another male adding to her trauma, he leaned back and bellowed his frustration. Praying for strength and calm, he paced in front of the truck.

He looked down as his phone beeped. It was a text message.

No trace of them. Cabin deserted. No scent.

Damn it. He wanted to sling his phone into the wall. Instead he called Nate.

"Yes, Alpha?"

"Calita was attacked tonight."

"Charles?"

Simon cursed. "I can't prove it. There was no scent. I'll get a description from Calita once I've calmed down. Find him anyway. His time in this town is up."

"What about his contacts?"

"We'll deal with it when the time comes."

He ended the call and stood next to the running truck, his mind full with thoughts of what could've happened to Calita. There was no space for anything else. Not consequence, not logistics for finding the person who attacked her…just her. Would they have killed her, or just hurt her? Hell, from his conversation with the elder, they didn't have to do anything other than menace his mate to accomplish their goal.

If destabilizing his clan was the goal.

The talk of it would get around town. Talk like that could easily cause chaos in their little town. Faith in the Alpha was what kept their clan so tight. Keeping the bears together was a struggle, especially since, by nature they were solitary creatures.

Not knowing who had hurt her was really messing with his head. It left him without a motive. Either way, he needed to calm his bear before he did anything else. It was riled, pissed, more so than he. He got back in the truck and pulled it around to the barn and parked it. He flexed his hands, his adrenaline still up from his fear. He'd thought having a mate would be easy, would be…simple. Calita was anything but. He wanted her implicit trust and it was hard being patient for it. He rubbed his forehead as his bear once again slammed against his mental shields. It wanted out, and it wanted their mate. It took everything in Simon not to rush inside and assert his dominance over his wary mate. He wanted, no needed, to feel her under him, submissive, knowing she belonged to him.

He'd never explicitly said she couldn't leave the house without him. But her carelessness in not having a phone irritated him. Especially in light of all her recent accidents. What had she been thinking? He sighed and opened the door. He could prolong going in by going to the cabin with Zeke, but his bear would tear through his control and he would be in his skin racing towards Calita. He walked to the main house with quick steps. He opened the door and set the alarm. Her scent led him to his bedroom and he was shocked. He expected to find her in the guest room, the walls in the house and in her heart once again blocking him from her.

He opened the door and she sat on the edge of the bed. Her head lifted, her fear and vulnerability there for anyone to see.

"I'm sorry," she whispered.

"For what, Cali?"

"Whatever you're mad at, I—"

He held up his hand to stop her. "I'm not mad at you, I'm mad at myself. You were nearly harmed, twice on my land. I'm mad because at every turn I've gone against my nature and asked you to do things my bear would rather demand. You walked almost three miles from this house, by yourself, with no one knowing where you'd gone. You weren't even on my land, Calita. I've asked you nicely to take it easy, you don't understand how hard it is for an alpha to ask."

Her face showed her surprise. "You're mad because I left the ranch alone?"

"Alone, and you were nearly taken from me in the process!"

She flinched and he sucked in a breath, turning away from her. His hands ached with the need to grab her, to kiss her. He wanted to leave his mark on her body, leave evidence for the world to see that she was his. But he knew with her history, that anything he did could reinforce the way her ex used to treat her. He was at a loss at how to treat her without further traumatizing her. His bear was near inconsolable that another bear had had its hands on her. He heard her clothing shift as she stood.

"Don't, Cali, don't come near me right now. I came upstairs to reassure you, but you can't touch me."

"What? Why not?"

The hurt in her voice turned him around and he shoved his hands deep in his jeans pocket to keep from reaching for her.

"Do you have any idea what you do to me, woman?"

"I apologized."

He growled, "Your apology sucked. It was rote, automatic."

She reared back. "Well excuse me, did I not grovel enough for you?"

"Calita, you're pushing."

Anger flushed her face. "So what? You're mad, and now you're going to pout about it."

"Pout? I'm trying to be sensitive to what you've dealt with from the piece of shit you dated. I'm trying to abide by the rules we set in this relationship, Calita."

"Rules you set." She stepped closer, her finger stabbing into his chest.

"Yes, rules I set. Rules that kept me from ravaging you. From locking you in this bedroom and fucking you until you agreed that you were mine," he shouted.

Her chest rose and fell in quick breaths but no panic infused her scent. "That's not, you can't just…"

"Can't just what, baby? Tell you what I feel? I'm trying not to push you, but it seems like every concession I've made for you only seems to get you in more danger."

She crossed her arms over her chest. "I didn't ask you to take it slow with me. You could have just left me alone."

"Calita, before you told me what happened to you, I was very much aware something haunted you. I've known you were my mate from the very second I smelled your scent. For a year I have been fighting the need to hunt you, fuck you, and mark you. Visceral needs, Calita. I've gone to bed every night yearning for you," he lowered his voice, his eyes meeting hers. "So no, I couldn't just leave you alone."

"Simon," she whispered, and stepped closer to him.

He stepped back. "Not yet, you can't touch me yet, my love."

"I'm sorry I didn't follow your safety protocols. It won't happen again."

He nodded. "Thank you for that. I need to go outside for a little while, I need skin time to soothe my bear."

Her hand reach for him again.

"Cali," he whispered. "Babe, I'm on the thinnest of threads here."

"What does that mean?"

"It means, sweetheart, that you scared the shit out of me. My bear is not feeling nice about it. I need skin time."

"You wouldn't hurt me, he wouldn't hurt me. You said that, everyone says that."

"You're absolutely right." He nodded. "But remember that conversation you asked me about, the day of the clan picnic."

Her eyes widened and her heartbeat kicked up.

"I need to let him settle a bit before I can touch you."

Her breath hitched, "if I'm your, your mate—"

His loud growl filled the room. "If?"

She lifted her hand and continued, ignoring his question. "You should let him do what he needs to do to calm down. I need to know if I can really do this, be what you need." Her voice was a whisper by the time she finished the sentence.

Hunger ripped through him and nearly sent him to his knees. His nostrils flared as he took in the scent of her arousal. He stepped closer, hands still in his pocket. She'd surely see them trembling if he took them out. He let his bear a little off the leash to test his mate. He leaned over and licked down her neck, needing to put his scent on her.

"Are you sure about this?"

Her body swayed and she nodded.

"I need words, Cali," he rumbled.

"Yes," she whispered.

Hands still in his pockets, he closed the distance between them until the hard points of her nipples poked into his chest. He closed his eyes and savored her scent, and the blast of heat flowing from her. He leaned over and kissed her neck, scrapping his teeth down the column. She whimpered and reach her hands to wrap around his neck.

"No," he ordered on a growl. "Leave your hands at your side. If you touch me, I stop." He bent his knees until his erection fit right between her legs. His bear bucked his control. *No, we'll take it easy on her this time. She's not ready yet,* he soothed his bear.

He pulled his hands from his pocket, and gave in to the need to touch her skin. His hands slid under her shirt, her smooth skin warm and soft. He pushed his hips up, grinding on the heat emanating from her center. She mewled and clutched her hands into fists. He kissed his way up her neck, pulling the lobe of her ear into his mouth.

"You can't imagine all the ways I want to take you, my sweet." He ran his thumbs over the peaks of her nipples, the lace of her bra no doubt adding to the sensation.

He rolled them both between his fingers, trailing kisses down to her collarbone. Her head lolled back.

"Please," she whispered. She moved her hips, grinding on his cock.

He smiled and allowed it. Of course, she would learn that he wouldn't always be so nice with his punishments. He trailed one of his hands lower, unbuttoning her jeans and slipping his fingers inside. Her body was scorching.

"My God, Cali, you're so wet, so hot. It's taking everything in me not to go down on my knees and devour you."

She gasped, her hips jerking as he slid aside her panties.

"You taste so good, and really, it's punishment for me not to be able to eat you."

She shuddered.

"This little button here," he pushed his thumb down and she moaned. "You remember, right, how I wrap my tongue around it?"

"Yes," her harsh whisper brushed his neck. She was gyrating her hips, moving her clit on his thumb, trying to reach the orgasm he felt tightening her body.

He pinched her nipple and pulled down on her clit and she hissed in pleasure. "Feel good, my love?"

"Yes!"

He took a kiss from her, spearing his tongue into her mouth, wishing he was driving it into her heat, tasting every drop flowing from her sex with his tongue. Her breath quickened and he smiled, pulling back from their kiss. He released her nipple next and she whimpered.

"Now, I'm going to give my bear skin time, and when we come back, depending on how nicely you apologize to your mate, I'll finish what we started."

He pulled his hand from her pants and she swayed. He kept his eye on her as he licked her taste off his fingers. He gave serious consideration to forgetting the dominance his bear needed, but seeing the defiance in his mate's eyes, he thought better of it.

"You can't do that."

He grabbed her chin and gave her a possessive kiss, sharing her taste. "If I come back here, and the scent of your orgasm is in the air, I will be very displeased. Take a shower, and whatever else you need to do to relax, but then I want you on our bed, undressed and ready for me. Am I clear?"

She growled. "You're serious?"

"Did you not stand here and tell me that as my mate you wanted to give my bear what it needed?"

"Yes, but I thought…"

"You thought wrong, sweetheart. It was either this or reddening that fine ass of yours. Would you have rather me pick the latter?"

She stepped back. "No."

He smiled. "As always, I leave it up to you. If I come back and you're in here sated, I'll leave it alone and sleep in one of the other guest rooms to give my bear space." He nipped her bottom lip. "Or, you can take your punishment like the strong mate I know you are, and get rewarded for your patience."

"That's not fair," she whispered, leaning into his body.

"I didn't say a thing about fair, love."

"How long will you be gone?"

He trailed a hand up her thigh, cupping his hand over her sex. She sucked in a breath.

"That's for you to find out." He backed away from her and out of the room, his bear satisfied that he was initiating their mate.

We go away from the house for skin time so we don't scare our mate, he warned his bear. He got a huff of disappointment as he started his shift, but his bear agreed. A little skin time, and then they could enjoy their mate.

– *16* –

Calita called herself every kind of fool as she lay naked on Simon's bed. The shower hadn't helped cool her off any. Her body still throbbed, her hands were shaking and she was feverish in her excitement. Simon threatened to spank her, and okay, she couldn't get into that, but the way he looked when he said it... She shuddered as another wave of need washed over her body. He'd slowly been becoming more dominant in their interactions, and when she examined that, she didn't have an issue with it. Was it weird that his dominance made her feel more secure?

She heard the front door open and then nothing. She tensed as the bedroom door opened. Simon stood there, his hair wild, and windblown, the smell of the forest on him and her body shot into heat. He growled, his pupils taking over his eyes, a dark black. Seemed he still wasn't in control of his bear. Simon stalked to her, his movements graceful, but no less predator. She shivered as his grumbling snarl sounded in the room. Her legs fell open, almost of their own accord. His eyes flashed, and a hungry smile tipped his lips.

"Mine," he growled and kneeled at the edge of his bed.

He tugged on her legs until she was on the very edge of the mattress, her sex exposed, and open to him. He licked his lips and she squirmed in anticipation. His gaze was intent, the concentration on his face sending a thrill through her. She threw back her head at his first lick to her folds. Her mouth parted as he made good on his promise to reward her patience. She gripped his hair, holding him in place as his tongue explored her sex.

Electric shocks traveled from her toes up to the top of her scalp as he devoured her. The orgasm that washed over her body threw her further into heat. Simon gave her no time to come down, instead, fitting his erection at her clenching center. He worked himself in, his chest rumbling with hungry growls. She spread her thighs wider, greedy for the feel of him. Simon's teeth scraped across her neck as he seated himself to the hilt inside of her.

"Fuck, Cali, the way you feel," he murmured as he thrust.

She forgot about her insecurities and fear with his every stroke. His heated whispers against her skin pulled her further under his spell. Keeping her feelings separate from him was never an option. She knew that now. She'd been naïve to think she could enter a relationship with this man and not fall for him. Simon nipped her chin and her eyes sprang open as he hit the spot inside that sent her reeling.

"There you are." His voice was barely a rumble.

Sweat dotted his forehead, and slicked their skin where they touched. She smoothed her hands down his back, lifting her hips to meet his every thrust. She bit her lip to keep her feelings from spilling from her mouth.

"Oh God," she whispered as another orgasm crashed over her.

Simon sealed their lips together, his body tightening as he followed her over the edge. He fell atop her, his body heavy in a way that felt secure. She gripped him tight, not allowing him to turn over. She wanted that weight for just a moment longer.

"I'm too heavy, love." He rolled them over.

***

She sighed and burrowed into his chest. Simon pushed his fingers through her hair and brought her closer to him for a kiss. His tongue tangled with hers slowly, his hands softly tracing her curves.

"I was worried about you," he whispered against her lips as they pulled apart.

"I know, I'll take better precautions." She traced his dark brows.

He nodded. "Can you describe the man who attacked you?"

She tensed, not wanting to talk about it while they lay naked. She sighed and rolled over, pulling her shirt off his floor. She pulled it over her head and sat up with her legs crossed under her, closing her eyes. She'd never forget the man's face.

"He was big, brown skin. His hair was cut low, his eyes were…" she shuddered. "Wide nose, large eyes, heavy brows. There was also a woman there."

Simon cursed and rolled onto his back. "Miranda." He turned back to her. "If you see the two of them again, I want you to go the other direction."

"You know who it is?"

"I think it's my ex-wife and her new mate."

Calita reared back. "Really?"

"He has contacts on the Oversight committee, so I've treated the situation as a nuisance. This is too far though."

"What are you going to do?"

"In the morning, I'll call Nate and deal with it." He reached for her and pulled her closer, his eyes glowing with hunger. "Right now, I'm going to enjoy having you safe in my arms."

He lifted her shirt and threw it back over his shoulder and slid his hands between her legs.

***

A week at Simon's house was spoiling Calita. What started out as only a couple days, had quickly changed once he got her in his bed. Each night when she brought up leaving, he'd talked her out of it. She shivered just remembering his hands caressing her as he convinced her to stay. She'd walked into her hotel room this morning and frowned at the impersonal space. She brushed her hair back from her forehead and considered how empty it felt. It really brought home to her that she'd been using this room as the last barrier to her committing to stay. She'd originally told Selena that she'd stay on a trial basis, but a year had passed and she'd refused to make a decision one way or another. Selena was amazing in that she didn't push her, but coming from Simon's place, she knew it was time to make that decision.

She had an appointment with Jerica and she needed something a little fancier than the jeans and t-shirts she'd carried with her to Simon's house. It was the only reason she was at the hotel. Being at his house had affirmed to her that she could no longer live out of a hotel. No matter that her friend wasn't making her pay for it. It was time she made moves to get her life back on track. Starting with a place to live, and a place for her bakery. She would take that step on faith and follow her dreams.

Jerica was going to show her shop spaces today and she was excited. She glanced at the brochures on her side table that she'd taken from the agent last week. She was still waffling about the apartment. Should she move in with Simon so soon? This mate business was outside of what she knew, and in the human world, moving into a man's house so soon wasn't done. She sighed.

Something to think about later.

A knock sounded at the door, so she dropped the brochures on the bed and went to answer. Simon stood there, sexy in a pair of fitted jeans and flannel shirt. He smiled and kissed her, pushing the door closed behind him with his foot.

"Hey, I was passing by and was told you were up here."

"Yeah, right," she wrapped her arms around his neck. "You were trying to catch me in the act of working."

"If you're trying to say that I'm looking for any reason to punish you, then you would be right."

She snorted. "I came to change. I have an appointment with Jerica. What are you doing in town?"

"Supply run." He frowned and backed up. "You're seeing the real estate agent? Why?"

She stepped from him and went into the closet to pick out a button down shirt. "Well, she's going to take me around to look at some spaces."

He was silent. She turned and saw him going through the brochures she'd left on the bed. "You're looking for an apartment?"

"Well…that's not... I wasn't sure about us."

"You already have one foot out the door with this relationship," he said softly.

"That's not true, Simon, It's time for me to get out of this hotel. To really start my life."

"And you can't do that with me?"

"With everything going on, I just…I didn't know if I was ready."

"Why won't you commit to this? I'm doing everything I can to let you know you can trust me."

"In fairness, I told you I wasn't ready for a relationship."

"And will you throw us away because you aren't ready?"

"That's not fair to ask, Simon."

"But I'm asking, Calita."

"You said you would give me time."

"You aren't giving me any indication that you're even considering my offer."

She sighed, "I am. It's hard."

He stood silent, his eyes going through emotions faster than she could track. The stubborn determination was there. He looked around her room. "I guess I should've known by the fact that you're still hiding in this hotel room that you weren't ready."

She sucked in a sharp breath, hurt at his dig. "That's fucking low."

Yes, she'd been thinking the same thing herself, but he'd said it to hurt her.

He shook his head and turned to leave. "You know where to find me when you've decided."

Anger bubbled to the surface. She wanted to lash out at him for leaving without even discussing it. "You promised me time. You can't get pissy because I'm taking longer than you thought," she snapped.

He growled, but stepped back taking a deep breath. "I'm not doing this with you."

All at once, one source of her insecurity revealed itself. They'd never last if he kept tiptoeing around her. Last night had revealed how much of himself he held back from her for fear of triggering her.

"Why, because I'm some fragile woman you have to treat like porcelain?" Lord, who had taken over her? What were the words leaving her mouth? Why was she challenging this man, knowing they were in this room alone?

"Why the hell are you coming at me for treating you better than the asshole you left? Would you rather I yell at you, force you to do what I want?" He took a step closer.

Stubbornness and anger kept her feet glued to their spot. She would not back down from him. "I would rather you treat me like a normal woman. Yes, I had this horrible thing happen to me, but you can't spend the rest of our life censoring yourself and your bear. It's not sustainable."

He stared at her for several breaths, his hands gripped at his side. "Have your ass home this evening. Don't make me come looking for you."

He stormed from the room and all the air left her body. She slumped to the floor, her heart damn near galloping up her throat. She pressed a hand to her chest. She'd done it. She'd stood up to him, and she'd seen none of the signs David had exhibited before he hit her. After a few moments to calm herself, she smiled. His last statement should've been taken as a threat. She could lie and say she wasn't turned on by it, but what was the point?

She chewed on that a bit as she stood to resume getting dressed. Simon was impatient with her, but, honestly how much time had he really given her to think about their relationship? A week, two? He needed to learn patience, alpha or no. He had to realize that mating would not come easy to her. Not like it did with the bears. They knew who their mates were as soon as they met them. She didn't have those instincts. Besides, she wasn't eager to get back into another situation where she'd lose herself. She didn't want the things David had done to follow her the rest of her life and ruin the chance she had to make something with Simon.

She growled into the empty room. She would be home as her mate ordered and that was that. How much longer would she lie to herself and deny them? She sighed and changed her shirt, determined to carry on with her plans. She needed to make her appointment with Jerica, then she would talk to Simon later.

***

Hours later, Simon was roaming around in his skin. He'd worked all day after leaving the hotel, or let Gavin tell it, he'd been sulking all day. His beta had had enough of his pouting and told him to take off. So Simon had spent the rest of the afternoon in his skin, playing in the lake, walking around and he was finally tired enough to go home and maybe sleep.

Maybe.

He wasn't angry with Calita, he couldn't be. She was right about the way he treated her. He'd had good intentions, but in trying to make her feel secure, he'd somehow made a misstep. The whole time he wandered in his skin, he'd mulled over their conversation. Were his parting words to her too much? Would they scare her off? He understood that she would have a harder time trusting, with what she'd gone through. Would she run to Jerrica and get an apartment? Damn it, he thought they had made better progress. He huffed out an impatient breath.

He'd overreacted to seeing the brochures. He would even begrudgingly admit to letting the talk around town get into his head. They knew Calita hadn't taken his bite, so speculation as to why was running rampant through Bear Ridge. Now that he thought about it, it was foolish the way he'd demanded her answer. He needed to call her and apologize.

First he'd take another dip in the lake. He paused when he reached the clearing, his nose high. He sped his steps, rushing to that familiar scent. He skidded in the dirt as he reached the picnic tables. Calita was sitting on top of a table, reading a book, dusk falling rapidly into night around her. She looked up as he got closer, a smile lighting her face. Hope started to bloom within his chest. His bear rushed to her and she set the book aside and reached her hands out for him. He chuffed as he slid his massive head between her legs. She rubbed his head as he butted against her stomach.

"Hi," she whispered.

He allowed his bear a few minutes with her, Calita's touch soothing them both. He changed forms, his nude body standing over their mate. Cali's eyes went bright with lust.

"What are you doing here?"

"Where else would I be, Simon? Did you not order me home this evening?" Her soft question had optimism rising.

"You didn't find an apartment?"

"I wasn't looking for apartments. I was looking for a spot to open a bakery."

"Really?" She'd shocked him again. "But the brochures."

"Yes, I had considered an apartment at one time. Jerica gave them to me a couple of weeks ago, even though she didn't think it would be necessary."

He held his breath. "And are they necessary?"

She stared at him for interminable moments. Moments that had his heart thumping. She took a deep breath.

"No, I don't think I'll need them."

He swooped down and kissed her. "What's changed since this morning?"

"Nothing," she said.

His heart plummeted.

She cupped his cheek. "I'm still scared of this relationship, and although it feels hasty, I'm willing to take that chance."

"But this morning—"

"This morning, you barged in and barely let me explain myself."

He sighed, and could admit to that. "So you've thought of my offer."

She rubbed her cheek against his. "I've thought of nothing else, Simon."

"And will you take it?"

"Do you plan on treating me like spun glass for the rest of our lives?"

He kissed her wrist. "My mate advised me that it wouldn't be sustainable."

She laid a gentle kiss against his lips. He deepened their kiss, allowing it to sooth his worries from earlier.

He pulled back. "Your answer, Calita."

"About becoming your mate?"

He growled. She was stalling and by the sparkling humor in her eyes, she was deliberately teasing him. He lifted her and lay her on top of the table, hovering over her.

"You're playing with fire, Calita."

She hummed and lifted her skirt, fitting her legs around his waist. "Does it warrant punishment?" she whispered.

"Lord have mercy," he whispered before devouring her mouth. "I won't make it back to the house before I have to have you."

"No one is asking you to."

He growled and ripped her panties, "Mine," he growled.

He positioned his shaft at the entrance of her sex. He paused, staring into her eyes. She smiled, and wrapped her arms securely around his neck.

"Yes." She pulled his head up for a kiss. "Make me yours."

He paused, he and bear both going still at her words. "Calita, that's…no teasing."

She lifted her hips until he'd sank into her sex. "No jokes, I want to be yours in every way that counts."

He chuffed against her neck, joy overwhelming him. He licked along the column of her throat and moved his head down, his hips driving in and out his mate, needing to feel her coming around him. Calita panted, scratched down his back and gave him back everything he poured into her. He nibbled at her shoulder, carefully considering where he wanted to put his mark. He slowed his strokes, savoring this first time he bit his mate.

Her channel flexed around his cock, pulling him out of his thoughts and under her spell. He bent his head and licked at her shoulder, fitting his mouth right at the crook and he bit down. She screamed, her sex gripping him tight as an orgasm toppled her. Power rose and filled him, their connection tightening, until he could feel her emotions and the sensation of her orgasm. It sent him into one that nearly made him black out. Still, he kept his hips moving as some of his power transferred from him, into Calita. She gasped, her back bowing, a second orgasm rocking through her body.

Simon snarled, his bear rose, and he sucked at his mark, shoving more of his hormone into it, strengthening both their bond and Calita. She whimpered, her body slowly relaxing as he pulled his teeth from her shoulder. He licked at the skin, sealing the wound. His throat tightened as his mark darkened, the teeth prints flattening, marring her skin like a birthmark.

He hugged her tight against his chest, kissing the mark, incredible pride surging through him. She was his, and with some of his power imbued within her, that much harder to hurt. It was the best protection he could offer her when she was away from him. Calita panted, her breath brushing his neck. Her slight discomfort filtered to him through their new bond. The night air was cool around them, the table surface hard against her back.

He cursed his carelessness. As a shifter, he hardly felt the temperature, but it wouldn't be the same for her.

Gathering her into his chest, he rolled them from the table. His bear was settled, secure now that Calita had his bite. Simon knew that it would change her body in ways that would make her stronger, heal faster, he was finally able to relax and it made him realized how tensed he'd been this whole year waiting on his mate.

"Bath?" He murmured against her mussed hair.

She sighed and wrapped her arms around his neck. "Yes, please."

He walked with her in his arms, the dark night wrapping around them. Her curves were pressed against him with his every step. He couldn't resist. He stopped and propped her against a tree. "You're mine now, Calita."

His cock filled, his bear's power saturating his body. He needed her. Again.

"All yours." She gave him a drowsy smile.

"I need to be in you." He whispered, pushing into her, giving action to his words.

Her walls tightened around him, giving him resistance as he pushed in. He kissed her, eating at her mouth, needing to be in every part of her he could reach. His strokes were slow as he held her up, their lovemaking only slightly less urgent than a few minutes ago. He reached his arm down and pinched her clit before licking against his mating mark. She moaned, low and long before gripping his erection with her sex, her back arching. He kissed her, swallowing her moans, still stroking her. Energized from his bear, he knew he could keep going all night. He'd show Calita just how well a bear treated its mate.

- *17* -

Calita stretched and rolled her eyes as she bumped against Simon's arm. She'd fallen asleep on his chest, but was not surprised to find herself on the other side of the bed, dangling on the narrow patch he'd left her. She'd figured out in the few days she'd stayed at his house that Simon was a wild sleeper. Even now, his massive body was splayed across the bed, nearly taking up the whole thing. She sighed and glanced at the clock. It was a little bit before five, just about the time she normally awoke to bake, so she slid her feet from under the covers and onto the plush carpet covering his floor.

It was time to get back into her routine. The few days at the ranch were already spoiling her. She shuffled from the bed, smiling at Simon's still sleeping body. He was so peaceful in rest. The energy was still there, but it seemed tame. She took a shower and headed down to the kitchen to make breakfast. Her phone beeped next to her. A good morning text from her father. She smiled. He was up earlier than usual. She bit her lip as she pushed through the dough, debating whether or not to tell them she'd been mated.

What would they say?

When she'd left Chicago, she'd been in a bad way. Barely leaving their house except for therapy. Only a year in this town and she felt like a different person. She was excited, happy about her mating and she wanted them to know. She wiped her hands and took a deep breath and decided to call.

Her mother answered and for a moment she froze. "Hello. Mom, hi."

"Calita, hi, we were just talking about you. How are you doing?"

"I'm doing well, actually."

"That's…" her mother paused. "I'm so happy to hear you say that. Have you been keeping up with your therapy sessions? It's been a year."

"Mom," she cut her off. "I haven't found a therapist here, but I decided to start looking."

Her mother let out a relieved breath.

"Mom," she whispered.

She and her mother had a relationship that was strained on some days, and awkward on the rest. Janet wanted to fix things, and Calita, according to her, liked to wallow.

Calita cleared her throat. "So, I… um, is dad there?"

"Oh, of course, I'm sure you called to talk to him."

"I…mom, I want to talk to you both."

Janet breathed and cleared her throat. "Oh. Ok." The phone went muffled and Janet called for her husband. "I have you on speaker, Calita."

"Hi, chef," was her dad's greeting.

Calita gave a watery laugh. Brian had always sounded so proud of her being a chef.

"I have news."

"Well, what is it?" Brian prodded.

"I'm mated."

There was silence on the other end.

"What does that mean?" Janet asked.

"Essentially, I'm married, but to a shifter."

More quiet.

"What kind of shifter?" Janet asked.

"Simon is a bear shifter."

"A bear?" Her father sounded startled.

"Does this mean there won't be a wedding?" Janet asked.

"Oh, well, I didn't think you guys would want…"

"Calita, why wouldn't we want you to do a wedding?"

"Really, dad, you want me to repeat verbatim your lecture to me on the patriarchy?"

"Well, I only said that so you wouldn't date until you were like, fifty, I didn't mean I didn't want to walk you down the aisle," he grumbled.

Calita laughed. "Mom?"

"Well, I'm happy for you, of course. I just, I'd really have liked to be there. It seems a little fast."

Her cheeks heated. "A mating isn't…you couldn't…" she stumbled.

"Oh, it's during sex."

"Brian!" Janet hissed.

"Well, that's what our daughter is trying to stutter her way through saying."

"We can have a wedding if you really want," Calita offered quickly, to get the subject off her and Simon having sex.

"Well, I don't want to pressure you," Janet cleared her throat. "I've talked some things over with your father and with my therapist and I realize that I have pushed you to do things that weren't for you."

"Mom," she whispered, her throat clogged. A tear fell. "You guys will love Simon," she said, changing the subject.

"I'm sure we will." Brian hastened to assure her.

"I've decided to open a bakery here."

"Oh honey, that's wonderful."

"That's so great," Janet said tearfully. "I know with the way things ended with David…"

Brian cleared his throat. "You've always wanted to bake, honey, I couldn't be happier. We'll come visit, when do you have some time?"

"I would love that. It's beautiful here. Very peaceful." She would keep recent events to herself.

She talked to her parents for nearly hour as she cooked, before hanging up. She felt unburdened and nowhere near as tense as she could sometimes get on the phone with her mother. It was…

Taking a deep cleansing breath, Calita went into the downstairs bathroom and splashed some water on her face and came back to finish her baking. It was still early and Simon hadn't yet waken.

Becca came in through the kitchen door, pausing to stare. She smiled, but that smile faltered slightly as the woman sniffed the air.

Calita gave her a polite smile and kept working.

"You're up early this morning."

Becca's irritation colored the air around her but Calita shrugged it aside.

"Well, I'm normally up this early, but the accident set me back a little."

Becca let out a huff and set her purse down on the counter. "You made breakfast."

"Just croissants and donuts. Simon's a little later than normal, I don't know that he'll want to eat anything big."

Becca walked over the refrigerator. "No matter when he leaves the house, he'll eventually come back to me and eat breakfast."

Calita shrugged and went back to the donuts she was frosting. She ignored the dig. Simon had marked her, in every sense of the word. She had hickeys in places no one would know. She wasn't worried about Becca. She looked up as she felt Simon enter the room. He didn't make a sound, and yet her body went on full alert in his presence. He prowled to her, his shirt unbuttoned and his jeans riding low. Heat suffused her body and she licked her lips.

He crowded her space, leaning over her mouth. "You beat me awake. Though not surprising, I barely got any sleep," he whispered before nibbling at her lips.

He coaxed her lips open, his tongue thoroughly exploring her mouth. She was breathless by the time he pulled away. He nuzzled into her neck, chuffing against her skin. She liked the sound. It was the same sound his bear made when it was near her.

"I don't have time for breakfast, riding fence line, see you for lunch?"

She shook her head. "I'm getting Zeke to take me into Selena's. Got pastries to make. Selena's getting grumbles from your bears."

She tensed, waiting on him to restrict her freedom now that they were technically married.

He kissed her neck. "Please be careful, love," he whispered in her ear, before he kissed her forehead.

"I made croissants, you can take them to go," she said, relieved.

He grabbed a napkin full of croissants and headed towards the mudroom where he kept his boots. She let out a breath, finished glazing the donuts and set them on a tray. She'd take it to the barn for the ranch hands before she left. She texted Zeke that she was ready. Becca went around the kitchen, she assumed making breakfast for the other ranch hands, like she did every morning.

"Would you like help?" She offered.

"It's my job," Becca gave her a fake smile.

Calita sighed. "Okay."

Zeke knocked a few minutes later. She gave him a tray of croissants and she grabbed the donuts. He smiled.

"These are not all for you. We're dropping them off at the barn."

"Boooo," He opened the door for her.

"Can I drive today?" She asked as they made the trek to the barn.

He frowned, "You got your car back?"

"No, but my insurance called and the car is totaled, of course. I need to get my nerve back before I buy a new car."

"That's fine with me. Want to take one of the smaller cars instead of the SUV?"

She blew out a raspberry. "Definitely."

A few minutes later, Calita sat behind the wheel of a small sedan, her hands gripping the steering wheel. Her breath was shaky as she stared ahead. Claustrophobia was settling on her shoulders, making her pulse pound loudly in her ears.

Zeke cleared his throat next to her. "I'm just going to turn the key so I can down the windows, no rush."

She gave him a wan smile as he pushed the button to down his window. Fresh air rushed into the car, and it helped. She took another shuddering breath and turned the key all the way. She could do this. The little car purred to life, the radio shouting out rap music, startling her. Zeke turned it down without a word. Silence once again blanketed the car. Tears clogged her throat as she realized she couldn't, in fact, do it. She couldn't put the car in drive. The thought of the stretches of backroad, where no one would find her if she had an accident had her chest tightening.

"I don't know if Simon told you this, but the cars from the ranch are lojacked." Zeke's voice cut into her panic attack.

"What?"

He settled in his seat, his shoulder against the door. "Yeah, so we can keep track of the vehicles. Alpha lets tourists use them sometimes and so we need a way to find them if they get lost out here."

She swallowed, loosening the stranglehold panic had on her throat. "No, I didn't know that."

Her shoulders loosened next as the full scope of what he said registered. Even if she was driving by herself, Simon would be able to find her. She wouldn't sit in a wrecked car with no help.

Zeke reached into his pocket and pulled out a small switchblade. Her hands shook.

"I want you to have this." His voice was nonchalant, but his eyes watched her carefully.

"I don't think…" Her thoughts drifted back to the night she was attacked. *Would having a weapon have made a difference?*

He put in in the cup holder between them. "It's small enough to fit in your pocket…you know, for emergencies."

Calita eyed it, her stomach roiling. For emergencies he said. Her gaze darted to him, but he was looking out of the window, his body relaxed. She could take the knife or not, it didn't seem to make a difference to him. Something else the women had shared with her on clan night occurred to her in that moment...

"Is it true that mates can share feelings, like tell what the other person is feeling?"

Zeke turned back to her and gave her an assessing glance, but nodded after a moment.

She sighed, relieved. If there was truly an emergency, then Simon would know. Oddly reassured, she put the car in reverse. She could, in fact, do this.

***

Simon checked the time on his watch, his mind, as always, on Calita. She'd been gone the whole day. He hadn't had time to dwell on it while he'd been working. His day had been spent as he'd told her earlier, riding the fence line and repairing any holes they found. He checked over some of the empty cabins to make sure they didn't need repair, and visited some of his more introverted bears. The government may have made laws that put them all in proximity to one another, but some of his bears still hadn't adapted. Yeah, they'd moved onto the Sanctuary, but they kept to themselves.

Once a month he and Gavin made it a point to visit them and make sure they had everything they needed. Every bear he'd come into contact with as he went about his day, sniffed at him and then offered congratulations. He knew the news would be all over town the moment Calita stepped foot into the diner. He was very happy about that. Gavin had teased him all day and was still at it as Simon dropped him off at the Beta cabin, done with their day. For all Gavin's ribbing, it didn't remove the smug smile Simon had worn on his face all day. Night had fallen and he was still smiling.

His phone beeped and he hoped it was a message from his mate telling him she'd made it home. He'd texted her earlier in the morning to make sure she'd made it into work, but hadn't heard anything else from her. It was a text from her saying that she would be a little late because she was packing her hotel room up.

Simon smiled, his bear excited. He realized that the text was hours old, which meant he'd missed it while he was out. Hopefully she wouldn't worry. As though a dam had burst, his phone started beeping with messages he'd missed while he'd been in the woods checking on his bears. He ignored them all when a call from Nate came through.

"Yeah?"

"Me and a deputy followed Charles and Miranda across the county line." Nate told him.

"Good. Any trouble?"

"Not so far. I'll keep you posted, of course."

"Thanks, Nate."

"Anytime, cousin."

Simon pulled his truck around to the parking spot where he normally parked and made the trek to the house, his heart lightened.

The smell of baking desserts greeted him as he sat down in the mudroom. His smile widened. Having Calita with him in the house was having some serious benefits.

He walked up on her as she was icing a cake. "You smell amazing." He inhaled at the side of her neck.

"You talking to me or the cake?"

He gripped her waist and brought her into his hard on. "What do you think?"

"I don't know, you could have a cake fetish."

He snorted, licking over his mating mark. "How was your day?"

She put down the utensil she was using and turned in his arms. "It was full of congratulations and gossip."

He sipped at her lips. "Any gossip I should know about?" Not that he cared, if it was important, it would filter back to him eventually.

"Well..."

He tuned her out as she launched into town gossip. The smell of her was rousing his bear, the animal caring only for wallowing in her scent. How amenable would their mate be to heading upstairs before dinner? He slid his hand under her shirt and closed his eyes. Her skin was soft under his calloused hands. Everything about Calita was soft, in all the best ways. She stopped talking and he looked up, his eyes hooded, drunk off her scent. She smiled and shook her head.

"You didn't hear anything I said."

He debated admitting that he'd zoned out, but instead changed the subject. "Did you clear out your hotel room, or do you need more help?"

She turned back to her cake. "I got everything. It was just clothes."

"Any regrets?" He forced his body to stay relaxed.

"No. Oh, I spoke to my parents earlier, we have to have a wedding."

"That's fine. It'll be fun, though I don't envy you the planning. The women in this town are likely to be all over it."

She snorted and handed him the bowl with a little bit of icing left. "I can't wait. Also, my parents want to visit so that they can meet you."

He scraped the side of the bowl with his finger, covering it with icing and made a line on her neck.

"Simon!"

He sucked on her neck, licking at the icing, hardening as her body went pliant beneath his hands. He bit down on her skin, leaving a mark and loving every part of it. He put another finger in the bowl. She squirmed in his arms.

"Don't you dare, Simon," she laughed and pushed away.

He caught her shirt as she tried to get away. They both looked up as Marcus, one of his enforcers knocked on the back door and entered.

Marcus grunted and he tensed.

"Where?"

Three short grunts was Marcus' answer. He cursed and gripped Calita.

"What's wrong?"

"Trespassing, eastern border of the property, I need to go check it out."

She tiptoed to kiss him. "Of course, I'll keep dinner in the oven for you."

"It may take a while, so eat if you get too hungry." He nuzzled into her neck.

She scoffed. "I'll be fine. Go." She pushed on his chest.

He gave her one last kiss and followed his enforcer out the back door.

***

Calita watched him leave, trepidation skittering through her stomach. She hadn't understood any of the grunting sounds Marcus made, but it was clear that Simon took it seriously. She went to wash the dishes to occupy her hands. Becca walked into the kitchen from the living room and pulled the roasted chicken she'd made from the oven.

"If you're done, Becca, you can leave. I'll clean up and everything." It would give her something to do.

Becca huffed and continued what she was doing.

"Is there a problem?" She'd been nothing but nice to the woman, she didn't understand her attitude.

Becca took off the apron she wore and hung it on the wall. "I don't have a problem."

"You know he's not yours, right?" It was impulsive, and honestly, Calita couldn't believe it had come out of her mouth.

"Yeah, well, you made sure of that." Becca turned her back and reached for her purse.

"Yeah, you can definitely go, and take your stank attitude with you."

Becca gave her a harsh stare right before the lights went out. The smell of smoke registered a moment later, and Calita's heart started racing. Smoke started to fill the kitchen and she pulled her shirt up over her mouth.

"Follow me!" Becca yelled into the darkness.

They raced for the back door, rushing from the house, not sure what part was on fire. She followed Becca into the forest behind the house, the same place she'd gone walking over a week ago. She knew walking too far would take her off the property, so she stopped. Becca kept going, and Calita turned back towards the house. No way was she getting lost in the woods again.

Becca probably knew the woods like the back of her hands, but she was too far away from Calita to follow. What should she do? It was dark as hell, and the light from the house didn't penetrate the darkness around her. She couldn't even make out the shape of the house from as far away as they were. She pulled out her phone to call Simon. A hand slapped over her mouth, a noxious smell going up her nose. She struggled for a few moments before everything went dark.

– *18* –

Simon rushed back to the house, with Marcus hot on his tail. Zeke was coming out of the kitchen, his face worried. Simon had felt worry from Calita through their mating bond a few minutes ago and ran back to the house. Seeing Zeke's face, his stomach dropped and his bear slammed against his shield around the animal. The smell of smoke was heavy on the air, the residual wisps of it rising from a trash can near the kitchen window.

"What happened?"

Zeke raked a hand over his shorn hair. "We got an alarm and rushed over. There was a small fire in that trash can by the kitchen window. The smoke was filling the kitchen when we ran up."

"Where's Cali?" he asked, his bear pushing against him.

Zeke's eyes went wide. "I didn't…"

Simon ran out into the back yard and screamed her name. He forced his body calm and took a deep breath, filtering through the scents on the night air. He growled as he caught both her scent and Becca's in the woods. "Spread out and look for her, Becca too."

He was panicked, but trying to keep it together. He pulled Gavin closer to him. "Call Nate, and get a crew together."

There was only the scent of Becca and Calita on the air. The two women couldn't have gone far, but what worried him was that he'd gotten Calita to promise him she'd never go too far from the house on this side of the property. What could make her go back on that promise?

***

Cali kept her body still, and her eyes closed. Her hands were tied behind her back, and a wooden floor was hard beneath her body. She blocked out the pain the position sent through her body and focused on the important questions. Namely, where was she? Last thing she remembered was a hand wrapping around her mouth. Who was it? And where was Becca?

"You're awake, no need in pretending." The voice was deep…familiar.

Fear was a hot lash through her body that sent her heart beat skittering. She cracked open an eyelid, and the guy who'd tried to take her a week ago stood over her, a smirk on his otherwise dark countenance. Besides the tilt of his lips, there was no amusement on his face. Just a resigned look that didn't bode well for her. She searched her mind for his name, Simon had warned her about him. She struggled to push herself into a sitting position, but he put his boot to her stomach.

He didn't press down, simply touched her with the tip of his toes. "Uh-uh. No need for all that."

She froze, but eased her body back onto the floor, wincing as her weight came down on her arms tucked behind her. "What do you want?"

He cocked his head to the side, and moved back from her. He pointed a single finger into the air… "That. That's what I want."

Calita heard her name called from outside, faint, but getting closer. She recognized Simon's voice, his panic seeming to bombard her already scared senses. Charles smiled at her and pulled her up by her hair. She screamed out and he laughed.

"Scream louder, Calita, your mate will come running all the faster."

Her fear nearly paralyzed her, until she thought on all that she'd gained since she'd moved to Georgia. She wasn't going to lose it, lose Simon. She wouldn't go out the way she did last time. She reached into her back pocket and palmed the small knife Zeke had given her.

***

Simon held his hand up to pause the crew following him. The four bears behind him skittered to a halt, their ears perking. The only sounds in the surrounding forest was that of their breathing. Even the night animals paused as bear shifters filled their romping area in search of their alpha female. A short scream rent the air and Simon growled low in his throat. He turned and pointed at one of the female bears with him.

"Get Nate and his deputies."

She nodded and took off.

He raised his nose and took a deep breath. "Calita," he hissed, and charged forward.

He stopped at the edge of a clearing as he got a look at Charles holding Calita at her throat. The bears behind him sent up a chorus of growls.

The side of Charles mouth tilted up. "I've been paid to take your alpha female, Jacobs, but I can be persuaded to give her back."

"What do you want?" Not that he had any plans to negotiate with the coward. He was only stalling until Nate could get there.

"My own land, for me and my mate."

"And I'm supposed to believe you would honor any deal made between us when you've already forsaken the deal you supposedly made to kidnap my mate?"

"One of your bears is undermining you, don't you want to know who?"

"You're bluffing." No way would he believe Charles over the bears in his clan.

"Not like you can tell." Charles smirked.

Simon was pissed because the male was right. Even as close as he was to Charles he couldn't smell him. "What's wrong Rossel? You've got family in the government, and they can't get land for you? Or don't they even acknowledge that they know you?"

Charles flinched and Simon knew he'd hit a sore spot.

"You have no idea who it is," Charles continued, directing the conversation back to the supposed traitor.

Rage danced through Simon. Even if there was no traitor, just the rumor that there was would undermine the security in his clan. His bear pushed against him, fur rippling up and down his arms, his teeth elongating as he met Calita's eyes. She was terrified, it was there easy to read, though the scent of it was slowly tapering off. He knew firsthand how easily she masked her feelings, but he was impressed. He watched her visibly compose herself, though it did nothing to soothe his beast. Simon's claws pierced through his skin, the need to eviscerate the threat to his mate uppermost in his mind. He had no plans to negotiate with the male. Charles would die, he decided. He was no longer waiting on Nate.

He was opening his mouth to say as much when Cali's body tensed. With movements quick for a human, she stabbed into the shifter's leg and swiped down. Blood saturated Charles pants and he roared, his claw piercing her neck. Simon watched in horror as the male's bear began its shift. Calita screamed, and pulled out her knife. Her next backwards stab missed its mark, but was enough to loosen Charles's hold on Calita's neck. She ducked and rolled out of the way.

Simon was on him not even a second later, his bear forcing its way out of his body. Even with Cali near and hurt, he had no trouble forcing the bear to concentrate on the fight with the trespasser. His bear wanted him dead, and with every swipe of his claws, he worked to finish the job Calita had started. Charles was starting to weaken and Simon heard a woman's scream. He couldn't let it distract him.

A weight slammed onto his back, and small human fingernails scratched at his fur. He shrugged her off, his determination to kill the male not wavering.

"No!" Miranda pushed between the two fighting males, diving on top of her mate in protection.

Simon pulled his claws back a scant second before they could touch his ex-wife. He didn't want to hurt Miranda, but he also didn't want the male to live. Simon's enforcers grabbed him, pulling him further from Charles before he could try again. Human laws forbade them from settling disagreements in the shifter manner, but the scent of the other male's blood was in the air, and Simon found it hard to pull back his bear. It was a fight, his human consciousness being pushed further back as the bear demanded its price.

Nate and his crew had rushed forward to help Charles as he lay on the ground. They hauled him up and rage had growls rumbling Simon's chest as he jerked against his enforcers' hold. He inhaled as deputies carried Charles from the clearing, a furious Miranda demanding medical care behind them.

Calita's scent surrounded Simon, bringing his attention back to her. He scanned the woods for her. She was being tended to by the clan females. Her body healing itself thanks to the transformation it had gone through when they'd mated.

"Simon," Calita stepped away from the women and came to him.

He shuddered at her hand on his chest, the bear allowing him more control. He scooped her up, careful of his claws and tucked her into him. He roared, the clan answering him back in pride and relief. He walked his mate the six miles back to his land, his bear not once relinquishing to Simon. Slowly her scent and the feel of her in his arms brought the animal's rage down. Once they got to his home and with every step up to his room, he shed his bear. By the time he'd reached the bathroom, he was nude, his erection jutting forward from the adrenaline and the feel of Calita in his arms.

She clung tightly to him, her body trembling. He set her down gingerly on the bathroom vanity and ran a warm bath. They were silent as he dumped in salts Anika had sent him some time ago to relax. The scent permeated the bathroom, his animal finally calming. He picked Calita back up and stepped into the tub. They were silent, letting the bath salts soothe both their emotions and their battered bodies. Her body relaxed on a shuddered breath, and a small hiccup. He kissed the top of her head.

***

Calita turned her head into Simon's chest. She hated the tears that tracked across her cheeks and landed on his chest, but damned if she could stop them. The possibility of what could've happened kept going through her head and she cried harder. Simon had rescued her, yes, but she knew the nightmares were coming. A part of her was relieved that she had defended herself, the other part couldn't help thinking about the violence she'd seen. Simon had nearly killed Charles, and it would be a while before she could get the image of his bear fighting out of her head. Simon said nothing, just held her tighter and soon the warmth of the water and his presence lulled her. She took a shaky breath.

"What will happen? I know shifter fights are illegal."

"That's not for you to worry about, love. Nathan will take care of Miranda and Charles and word of what happened won't leave this town."

"You don't mean—"

"No," he hastily reassured her. "No. He won't be killed. Now that the heat of the bear is not riding me, I'm glad I stopped. Nate will hold him and tomorrow morning I'll handle it."

"What if he tells the council?"

He sighed and kissed the top of her head, and snuggled her closer. "Put it from your mind. As it is, you're already going to have a hard time sleeping. Let it go and let me take care of you tonight."

She nodded, happy to have one less thing to add to her nightmare reel tonight.

- 19 -

Calita yawned as she pulled together ingredients for biscuits. She had sausages going on the stovetop and eggs already settled into one of the warmers Simon had. She looked at the oven time again and frowned. Becca was late. After the woman had disappeared on her last night, she shouldn't care, but a part of her wanted to be sure she was okay. Calita had started breakfast knowing the woman would give her a look when she arrived, but she needed something to do with her hands.

Cooking was how Calita always cleared her mind, and this morning she needed it. She would simply ignore the loud sighs and eye rolls Becca was sure to give her when she came in.

Last night, despite what she'd thought, she hadn't had any nightmares. Of course, she'd barely shut her mind off enough to actually sleep for more than three hours, so that could've been why. She'd given up trying to go back to sleep an hour ago and had joined Simon in the shower when he woke. It was still dark outside, but Simon had went out to do whatever it was that ranchers did this early in the morning. She gently mixed in her biscuit ingredients and looked around Simon's house.

What else did Becca do for him? She knew the woman cooked for him. Did she clean? That was something Calita would definitely not be doing. She hated cleaning. It was the best thing about staying in the hotel for as long as she had. She shoved the biscuits in the oven as she heard the back door open. Simon came in, and smiled, his gaze raking over her face.

"Mate," he growled and kissed her deeply.

"I'm going into work," she announced as he backed up.

"Are you sure?" He asked, cupping her cheek.

She nodded. Granted, she'd literally just thought of it, but yeah… "I'm sure, love. But…I did want to talk to you about something."

He sat at the island and pulled her into his lap. "What is it?"

"I was thinking about what you said about one foot in. Now that I know I'll be in Bear Ridge for the long run, I needed to make long term plans."

"And," he grabbed her around the waist.

"I want to bake. I mean, I know I do it already for Selena, but, I'm going to open my bakery."

He smiled, pride lighting his eyes. "That sounds amazing, I'll do whatever I can to help."

A tide of relief flooded her and she kissed him. She stood as the timer on the stove beeped. "Then, I'll talk to Selena today about it."

"You can ride with me into town."

Right, he had to go to the sheriff's office. Her nerves skittered across her skin as she thought about last night. Simon and the town could get in trouble for what happened last night. She flipped the sausages on the stove.

"What will happen, will the committee get involved?"

"Not if I can help it," he sighed.

Worry coated the kitchen and stood between them as they went through breakfast. When it was clear that Becca wasn't showing up, Simon called her but didn't get an answer. A part of him was worried, but there was nothing he could do about it until he handled the immediate problem of Charles.

He helped Calita clean the kitchen, and set up the rest of breakfast for the ranch hands. Once done, they headed to the garage.

"What are you going to do?" She wrung her hands.

"About Becca?" He handed her into the cab of his truck.

"No, Charles and Miranda."

He ran around the front of the truck and slid into his side. "I called the clan lawyers this morning. I'll meet with them and draw up paperwork that bans the two of them from our county."

"What if he doesn't sign it?" She worried her bottom lip.

He was silent a moment as he started the truck. "Then I'll press kidnapping charges and a litany of any other things the lawyers can make stick."

"If he has contacts—"

"Love." He interrupted her. "I don't want you to stress about it."

"Well, I'm your mate, so there won't be any of this patting the good little wife on the top of the head stuff, just so you know."

He chuckled. "Fine. I'll let you know what happens later."

"Fine," she said and turned her attention to the passing scenery.

***

Although Simon been in a meeting with the clan's lawyers for hours, Calita was the only thing on his mind. She hadn't said anything to him, but he knew she'd barely slept last night. She'd tossed and turned in their bed, snuggling every once in a while, clutching him tight. He'd worried that she would have nightmares after what happened yesterday, but he hadn't thought about her not sleeping. He sent her a text message to check in with her.

"Simon."

He looked up to three pair of eyes on him. "Sorry, yeah?"

"I was saying, Charles is already healed, and it will be his word against yours if he decides to push back on the kidnapping."

"I don't want the committee in this county, never mind the town. Make sure whatever we do sticks." He stood, done with the conversation.

"Yes, Alpha." All three lawyers scrambled behind him.

"Call ahead to Nate, we can give Charles his options."

They rode behind him as he headed for the center of town and the sheriff's office. Nate met him at the door.

"I have him and Miranda next to each other." His cousin inclined his chin to the lawyers coming up the stairs behind him. "They work it out?"

"So they say," Simon murmured.

Nate walked the four of them back to the cells and left them at the door of the jail. Simon walked straight to Charles' cell, giving Miranda a cursory glance in the cell next to him. He ignored her tear streaked face and focused on her mate.

"You can't do this to us," Miranda hissed.

"You came onto my land and tried to take my mate. You've been spreading rumors—rumors that could cause trouble for my clan—be glad I haven't done worse than this," he growled at his ex-wife.

"We used to fight side by side. I can't believe you would turn your back on all of that." Miranda gripped the bars.

Anger welled in his chest. "I turned my back? That's rich coming from you."

One of his lawyers cleared their throat.

He turned his gaze back Charles. The arrogant jackass was sitting with his head leaned against the wall. Why had they risked coming to his town? It was on the tip of his tongue to ask, but then, from the information the lawyers had dug up, Charles and Miranda were running out of places to land. At least places with clans. The pair had long been kicked out of the Rossel family clan.

The male smirked. "You don't know the trouble you're inviting."

Simon grunted and crossed his arms over his chest. "Oh, do you think Eldred Rossel is coming to your rescue?"

His bear wanted to tear the bars off the jail and beat Charles with them, but he was forced to deal with the situation in the way the government laid out. He grit his teeth as he stared at the male who had tried to hurt Calita.

One of the lawyers stepped forward and passed a sheet of paper through the bars. "Mr. Rossel, I have a statement from your uncle here."

Charles stared at it for long moments before he snatched it from the lawyer's hand. His face went hard, anger darkening his eyes. He crushed the paper. "You can't keep us here."

"I don't want you here," Simon nodded to the lawyers; they passed Charles another sheath of papers. "I'll give you an hour to look over this banishment paperwork. I was even nice enough to bring in a lawyer from the next town so there's no conflict of interest. He'll go over it with you and your mate, and when that hour is up, you will leave Clarke County and never come back."

Miranda moved closer to the bars in her cell. "Charles, what is he saying? We can't get kicked out of another town."

"Stop it, Miranda," Charles barked.

"This was the last clan—"

"Enough," Charles hissed.

"Simon, please." Miranda turned back to him.

"Why would you risk it?" Curiosity wouldn't let him leave it alone.

"I was serious about needing to lay low. This time we bit off more a little more than we—"

"Shut.up.mate!" Charles said between clenched teeth.

Simon spared the male another look, the anger in Charles eyes swaying him no more than the desperation in Miranda's. He knew the work that they did as part of the resistance. Some of it wasn't legal, and there were times when avoiding law was the difference between life and death. He was no longer in that life, and he'd not let Miranda drag him back into it. He had too much to lose.

Simon shook his head and turned his back, walking over to the lawyer waiting at the door. "You can go in and consult with your client," he told the anxious male.

Gavin was waiting for him on the other side of the door. "Did you ask about the traitor?"

"There is no traitor." Simon let out an irritated sigh.

"Becca is missing." Gavin changed the subject knowing his alpha well enough to know not to push.

"Missing?" She hadn't answered his call this morning, but he had pushed it to the back of his mind, wanting to deal with Charles.

"I went in to check on her after I didn't see her at breakfast. She hasn't been answering her phone all morning."

Nate walked up to them both, his face bunched into a scowl. "We finally found the car that hit Cali."

- 20 -

"Are you sure?"

Calita cut her eyes at Selena as they both wandered the empty store front. "I'm positive."

Selena sighed and walked over to the large window facing the street. "It's a great location."

"Isn't it." She spun in a circle. Already her mind was full with décor ideas.

"I supposed you'll want Anna to come with you."

Calita went over to Selena and hugged her friend from behind, smiling at her pout. "She's got a knack."

Selena pat her arms. "I'm happy for you, Calita. When you came here a year ago..." She spun and stared, her eyes wet. "I thought I'd never get my friend back."

Calita cleared her throat and stepped back. "I'll never be like I was, Selena."

"And that's fine," Selena rushed to assure her. "I just…David took a lot from you, I'm happy to see you getting some of it back."

"I know what you mean." Calita whispered. "I should have listened to you."

"It doesn't matter now."

Calita nodded and walked over to the counter. "The store was built to be retail." She wiped the corner of her eyes and changed the subject. "I'll have to make a lot of changes."

Selena pat the tears from her own cheeks. "I know some people."

"In this town," Calita snorted. "I'm sure you know everyone. The builder said he could expand the kitchen. I'm waiting on a price for it."

"I'm sure Simon won't mind paying."

"I'm doing this myself. I have savings, and I can get a business loan for the rest."

Selena raised an eyebrow. "Well, look at you. I guess I'll have to get a new kitchen manager."

Calita laughed, happy the tension was breaking. "I never officially accepted that job. I was supposed to be just kitchen help."

"I tried." Her best friend shrugged. "This will be great, Cali."

"I think so too."

***

"Are you sure?" Simon held onto the bar above the window of the passenger side as Gavin took another corner on two wheels."

"Damnit, Gavin, slow the hell down," Nate shouted from the back. "I should be the one driving. I'm the sheriff."

"I am not bumping around in that ancient jeep you love," Gavin shot back.

"To answer your question, yes, we're sure," Nate said before checking to be sure his deputies were still behind them.

"Why?" Simon turned to look at his cousin.

Nate shrugged. "We'll find out shortly."

Gavin slowed as they turned off the main road onto a dirt road. He pulled his truck into a nicely kempt yard where a small sedan sat caddy corner to the front door, its trunk open.

"Looks like we got here just in time." Simon cursed and pushed the door open as Gavin pulled up.

A woman froze as she came to the door of the small ranch style house, her eyes darting to the side where a covered car was parked. Nate headed to the car, but Simon kept his eyes on the female.

"Alpha." Tessa moistened her lips, her gaze pinging between them and the deputy's car coming up behind them in the drive.

Nate whipped the cover from the car and revealed a blue sedan, the front end damaged. They all stared at the woman.

"Something you want to explain, Tessa?" Simon's voice deepened, his bear suffusing his body with power.

"She wasn't supposed to get hurt. Just run out of town." Tessa put the suitcase she was toting on the step and sat down beside it.

"You ran my mate off the road. She could've been killed!" His voice echoed in the surrounding forest.

Tessa bared her neck, tears cresting her cheeks. "I wasn't the one driving the car. I just gave her the message. She was never supposed to be hurt."

"Out with all of it. Now." Simon clenched his hands at his side. He didn't dare take a step close to the female.

Not that he would put a hand on her, but his bear wanted her submission, and between the animals, he wasn't sure what would happen.

She wiped a hand down her face. "Becca called me and said that Calita was taking you from her. I was just supposed to make sure she was headed away from town."

Nate grunted. "Towards that dead zone. What did you think would happen to her?"

"Becca said she would just talk to her, that's it, I swear."

Simon's heart thumped against his ribs. "Becca was driving the car?" He staggered back, shock blanching away his anger.

She nodded. "We…the rumors around town. I helped her with that, but that was it," she whispered.

"You've been undermining this clan?" Gavin stepped closer to the female.

Nate put an arm out to stop him. "Where is Becca?"

Tessa sniffled and wiped her eyes. "We're supposed to meet in Pleasant Hill and leave the state together."

"No other clan anywhere near here will take you. I'll make sure of it," Simon swore softly.

She gasped and lowered her head. "I told Becca we would be banished. She was so desperate."

"What in the world would she gain?" Nate asked.

"She wanted Simon to herself."

"I'm mated." Simon was confused.

Tessa shrugged. "If she could get Calita to leave before you mated her, then there would be no one for you, but her."

"What the hell?" Gavin stormed off.

"Calita," he whispered. "Where is Becca now?" A sense of urgency started to fill him.

He didn't wait for the answer, he rushed to Gavin's truck. Nate ran behind him, instructing one of his deputies to stay with Tessa. Gavin hopped in and kicked up dirt as he sped out of her driveway. Simon pulled his phone out and dialed Calita's number. He cursed as it rang until the voicemail picked up.

"Faster, Gavin," he implored.

His Beta floored it, and the truck spit out onto the highway, leaving a cloud of dust behind them as they sped away.

***

Calita perused the back room, doing mental calculations. She'd have to get the builder to enlarge the room back here as well. A bigger place to store her supplies would be needed. She smiled and ran her hand across the wall. She was doing it. She was going to open her own bakery. She couldn't wait to call her father and tell him. She'd also get him to send her the recipe book that she'd left at their house. It was full of recipes that had been passed down from his side of the family. Over the years, she'd tweaked them to suit her, making them fancy as her father had complained. Her phone went off in the other room, so she backed out of the storage closet.

"You know, Selena, you can still order your morning pastries from me." Calita paused as she rounded the corner to the front of the store.

Becca stood there with a gun trained on Selena. Her phone went silent for a second then started ringing again, vibrating across the counter. It broke her stupor.

"Becca. What are you doing here?"

Becca swung the gun on her. Her face was splotchy, her eyes red-rimmed. "You ruined everything."

Calita raised her hands. "I haven't done anything to you."

"He was supposed to be mine."

"You know that's not how mating works, Becca," Selena said softly.

"He was mine. He wasn't looking for a mate." Becca's hand shook as she brought the gun higher.

Her focus was solely on Calita. Becca's rage-filled eyes raked her face with a sneer. Calita's heartbeat stuttered. Would she die here right on the cusp of getting her dreams? She reached for her connection with Simon, needed to feel him if it would be her last few minutes on Earth. She felt his desperation, his fury. She sent him her love in return.

"You don't have to do this, Becca." Calita kept her voice calm and forced her heartbeat to slow.

"It should be me. I took care of him when Miranda left. I helped him take care of his father as he lay dying. I was there for him! You can't just come in take what I worked for."

Calita kept her body from tensing as Selena moved. She looked into Becca's eyes, keeping her attention. "You've done so much for him. I know that."

"Then you know you don't deserve him," the woman whispered.

"I didn't intend to take anything from you," she insisted loudly to cover up Selena's movement.

"If I can't have him, you shouldn't be able to either." Becca's arm holding the pistol steadied.

The world around Cali slowed down as the woman bit her lip, her face calming as she aimed the pistol. Becca's words resonated, and reminded Calita of another time, another person who'd claimed if he couldn't have her no one else could. Anger started to fill her, battling with desperation. Unbidden, her gaze shot to Selena as her best friend lifted a small step stool and raised it over her head. Becca saw Calita's eye flicker to behind her. She swung to look as Selena brought the stool down on her shoulder. The gun went off before clattering to the ground. Becca screamed and Selena raised the stool again. Calita didn't think, she simply tackled Becca before she could attack her friend.

They hit the floor hard, wrestling. Becca screeched and grabbed her hair. Calita didn't bother with hair pulling, she punched the woman as hard as she could in the face. She landed blows any way she could, scrambling across the tile floor with the woman. She cursed as they bumped into the gun, sending it scurrying across the floor. Selena picked it up and leveled it at them. Still, they fought.

Calita knew if she stopped, Becca could overpower her in seconds. She didn't know how long they fought on the floor, all she knew was that she was done being a victim. Fur exploded along Becca's arm, the wild smell of bear permeated the air and Calita cursed. No way could she take a three hundred pound bear if Becca changed.

She fought harder, hoping to disable Becca before she could fully transform. The gun went off and both women froze. Selena lowered her arm from the ceiling and pointed it at Becca, breathing hard.

"If you shift, I'll shoot."

Calita slipped as she sought purchase on the tile, banging her knee against the hard floor. She rushed to her friend's side, wanting to be on the other end of the gun in case Selena made good on her promise.

Becca growled and seemed to consider it. After a moment, she stood and charged them both, fur exploding all over her body as her bear form took over. Selena fired but it didn't slow the bear as it crashed into them, sending them into one of the counters. Cali shook away her shock and kicked out, fighting for her very life. Calita heard her name being called vaguely before she was hauled up, arms banding around her waist. She didn't stop fighting, she still swung. Nate growled into Becca's face, his bear ripping through his clothes. He pulled her up, grabbing and spinning her around away from Calita.

"It's over, love. It's over." Simon pulled Cali's head into his chest, his forehead on the top of her head. "Calm yourself, baby."

Calita clutched him, adrenaline still spiking through her system. Pride was there, mingled in with the fear. She hadn't laid down, she'd fought for her life, unlike last time.

"She was going to kill me."

Simon gripped her tighter. She looked up as one of Nate's deputies grabbed the gun from the floor and unarmed it, tucking it into an evidence bag. Another deputy led Becca from the shop, her arms handcuffed behind her back, a blanket wrapped around her nude body. Calita searched for Selena and found her bundled into her mate. Nate's face was hard, his normally stoic countenance suffused with fury, his hair in disarray as he gripped Selena, tucking her under his blanket. The fact that she could've died settled on Calita's shoulders and then the trembles started.

"I have you, love," Simon whispered, settling on the floor with her still in his arms.

"I want to go home," she whispered.

"In a minute. I just…I need a minute to hold you." Simon rained kisses along her face and neck.

***

Hours later, the scent of herbs greeted him at the bedroom door. He knew his cousin had come to visit Calita, and from the scent emanating from their bathroom, Anika had left gifts for his mate. He followed the scent into his bathroom and leaned on the door jamb, watching Calita. She was toweling off, her hair high in a bun. She turned and gasped as she spotted him. She clutched the towel tied around her chest.

"Is it done?"

Simon walked over to her and sat her on the vanity, stepping between her legs. "She's in our jail, awaiting transport tomorrow morning for arraignment."

"Will she go to shifter prison?" Calita released her hair and he lost his train of thought as he watched it cascade down her shoulders and back.

He grabbed a few strands, bringing it up to his nose. He closed his eyes and reveled in the scent. He dropped her hair and nuzzled into her neck, licking at her still wet skin.

"Simon?" Her breath caressed his neck.

He shuddered, need for her welling inside him. "Yes, love?"

"Becca, will she go to jail?"

He lifted his head and cupped her cheeks. He dropped small kisses across her lips and jaw. "Yes, attempted murder carries weight, and I have no plans to intervene. She'll serve her time somewhere other than Bear Ridge, and she's been banished from this clan."

She touched her forehead to his. "I feel bad that she'll lose her home."

"It's on her, Cali. The bond between mates is sacred. She made her choices."

Simon felt no guilt or remorse for having her arrested. His bear wanted to handle it in a far more barbaric way, but banishing her to her bear's body was cruel. He sighed and dropped a kiss behind Calita's ear.

"Can we be done talking about this?"

"You have better things to discuss?" She asked softly, pulling him tighter into her body.

"Better things to do for sure," he murmured against her lips.

She wrapped her arms around his neck. "I had hoped you'd join me in the shower."

He growled and released the towel from her breasts. He watched her face to make sure she was still comfortable. None of the trepidation she used to have at him seeing her nude was visible on her face. He caught her gaze watching him, concentration, and heat flitting in her eyes.

"You are so beautiful to me." He kissed her, pulling her into his body.

"You make me feel that way," she told him as she lifted his shirt. "Now, come out of these clothes."

His smile spread across his face at her greedy hands. "Is there something you need?"

She growled and pulled her bottom lip between her teeth.

He laughed and pushed his pants down, his erection jutting forward. Her eyes went wide with lust. She licked her lips. Her gaze made him feel like a god. His chest swelled and a powerful need over took his body. He pulled her to the edge of the vanity.

"Tell me you love me," he demanded, pushing into her wet sex.

She flexed around him and his muscles tightened, the need to pound into Calita dimming his vision until only she stood out.

She arched her back, her channel squeezing around him. He hissed, his hips jerking, burying his cock all the way to the hilt. She smiled, a devilish smile that he would spend the rest of his days giving her a reason to recreate.

"I love you, Simon. Now, no more talk, I want sex."

Epilogue

Calita kept her body still, despite the nerves rioting underneath her skin. She squinted, watching the end of the driveway. Simon fidgeted next to her as a dust cloud appeared in the distance. She bit her lip and barely stopped herself from bouncing from side to side.

"Stop it, you look amazing," she said absently as her mate fiddled with the sleeves of his flannel shirt.

"Your parents are college professors, maybe they will think I'm a rube because I own a ranch. I should've worn something else."

She snorted. It was cute how nervous he was. She'd never seen him any other way than self-assured. She smiled, one mention of meeting her parents and he'd instantly changed before her eyes. She wanted to lie to him and say her parents weren't academic snobs, but he would see through the lie. Though, it could resort in a punishment which…she considered it.

"You'll do fine. They'll love you," she said instead.

"Will your mother launch into wedding talk immediately?"

She laughed and pat his chest. "Possibly."

"And your dad?"

"My daddy…" she sighed, her smile dropping. "He'll be a little hard. David did a number on our instincts."

Simon pulled her into his chest and kissed the top of her head. "Everything that happened brought you to me." He reminded her.

She wrapped her arms around him tight. The car that had been steadily getting closer, pulled up and she separated from Simon, nearly skipping down the steps. Simon was right behind her. She knew he would be. He'd always be behind her. He'd helped her through the months of construction required to get her bakery to her specifications. Their only hiccup when she wouldn't allow him to pay for it. He'd still gone behind her back and took some of the costs off her, but she'd taken him to task and it hadn't happened again.

He was good like that, listening and adjusting to what she needed.

She reached back and grabbed his hand and they waited as the car parked. Her mother stepped from the passenger side of the car they'd rented, a happy smile on her face. Calita had offered to pick them up from the airport in Atlanta, but her parents had spent two days in the city before coming up to Bear Ridge. Calita squeezed Simon's hand and rushed to her mother, so excited to see her.

Janet hugged Calita then cupped her cheeks. "You look so happy," she whispered.

"I belong here, mom."

Janet nodded and stepped back. Calita rushed to the driver's side and embraced her father.

"Be nice, dad."

Brian merely grunted and squeezed her tight. She led her father to the front of the car by the hand. "Dad, Mom, this is my mate, Simon Jacobs. Simon, this is Doctors Brian and Janet Wright."

Simon smiled and held out his hand. Simon's face was nervous, but open, his happiness at meeting her parents obvious. Her world tilted a moment before righting itself. She loved him, more in this moment than she thought was possible. She swallowed the lump in her throat. A year ago she hadn't thought this happiness was possible.

"It's nice to meet you both." Simon's deep voice brought her thoughts back to them.

"This is an impressive spread," Brian commented.

"I can't wait to see the horses," Janet's eyes took in everything.

"Of course, I have a couple gentle mares set aside for a tour after Calita's opening."

"The opening!" Janet clapped her hands. "I'm so excited for you, honey. I can't wait to see what you've done with the place." Her mother tucked her hand under her elbow and led her towards the house. "The boys can get the bags, you tell me everything. The pictures you sent of the before had me worried."

***

Simon watched his mate walk up the steps with her mother. Calita looked exactly like the older woman, down to their gait as they walked away. He turned back to the car to find her father studying him.

"I did some research on bears."

"Is that right?"

Brian nodded. "Enough to know what it would take to bring a clan such as yours together." His eyes assessed the ranch before settling back on Simon. "I'm told a mate is gold to shifters," he said softly.

"Calita is the other half of my soul," Simon told her father, his voice earnest, conveying the truth of his words.

Brian gave a worried look towards the house. "Well, we'll see what's what. Let's get the luggage out, shall we?"

Simon nodded, knowing that's all he could expect from a man that had watched his daughter go through hell and come out the other side. They carried the luggage in. Simon guided him to the downstairs guest bedroom that her parents would be using. Calita and Janet were cooing over the antique furniture. He could only stare in wonder as he watched his mate brag to her parents about him preserving his family history.

Her mother gave him a pleased look. "A man who appreciates where he comes from. I like it."

He dropped their luggage just inside the door. "I'll let you guys get settled, and then I'd love to take you on a tour of the town?"

"We'd love that," Brian agreed.

Calita gave them a hug and then followed Simon from the room. They ended up in the living room on the sofa, facing his big screen TV.

"I think they like you," she said, bumping his shoulder with her own.

"They gave me you, I'll love them."

She smiled and pulled his head down for a kiss. "I love you so much," she whispered into his mouth.

"I'll love you forever," was his reply.

He kissed her, so happy she was in his life.

About the Author

I am a full time photographer, and a mom of two. I've been writing my whole life, and after the birth of my first kid, I decided I couldn't very well bring up a fearless human without first trying the things that scared me. So, I wrote my first book, and then subsequently more.

I write stories that I've always wanted to read: love stories that feature brown girls like me. I love the thought of fantastical creatures and worlds where anything is possible and that's what I bring in my stories.

My website, where you can get news and sneak peeks of upcoming books: http://www.driaandersen.com/

Other titles by Dria Andersen

Destiny Series

A Destiny Awakened

A Destiny Revealed

Haven Series

Haven

Soul Bonded

Standalone Paranormal Titles

Chasing Savannah